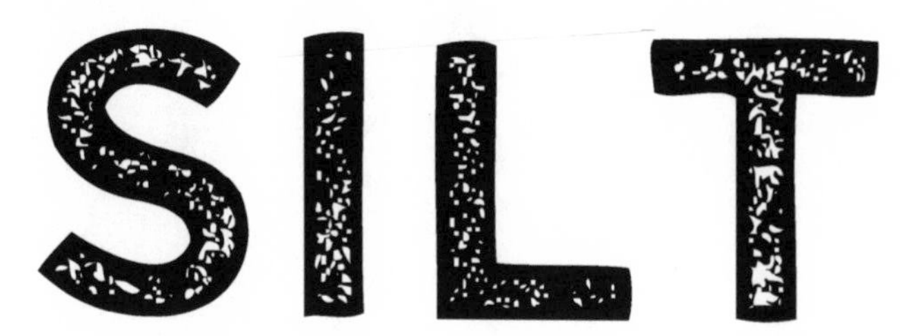
SILT

Ein Hard-Boiled Spiel

A Novella

CHRIS GEIER

Alternating Current Press
Boulder, Colorado

Silt
Chris Geier

Alternating Current
Boulder, Colorado
alternatingcurrentarts.com

ISBN: 978-1-946580-13-9
First Edition: March 2020

ADVANCE PRAISE

"So much packed into such a compact length: an engrossing hard-boiled detective yarn, a rich evocation of 19th-century Ohio in all its discontents, and a meditation, finally, on what it means to be American. With its singing prose and gripping story, *Silt* is an accomplished debut, and Chris Geier is a writer to watch."

—Louis Bayard,
author of *Courting Mr. Lincoln*

"Geier gives us a vividly savage Cincinnati of 1856 and a uniquely vicious bounty hunter to navigate it, Werner Bosenbach, "the Dutchman." The balance of gritty, historical detail that mires the reader in the setting's filth and a bloody pacing that intensifies the suspense makes *Silt* an arresting novella."

—Kevin Catalano,
author of *Where the Sun Shines Out*

"Geier is a storyteller whose work is rooted in history, but it's not the history we know. His characters have the distanced authenticity of our friends-of-friends, the woman so-and-so told you about, from that place that one time. Their dilemmas lie in the spaces between their desires, consciences, and capabilities, and Geier displays their secrets like trinkets in a shop window, showing us their most intriguing angles to draw us in. *Silt* is a hell of a read."

—Schuler Benson,
author of *The Poor Man's Guide to an Affordable, Painless Suicide*

"Chris Geier packs one hell of a story into these pages—a thrilling, alcohol-fueled tour of 1850s Cincinnati, brimming with lush details and larger-than-life characters. *Silt* goes down like a slug of good whiskey—smooth, with just the right amount of burn."

—Sara Rauch,
author of *What Shines from It*

THE SPIEL

For my parents.

"Woe to all the just and merciful in the land."

—Frederick Douglass, 1850

SILT

1
The Widow

June 1856

From the southern banks of the Ohio River, he looked back at Cincinnati. Smudged by summer mist, the city was penned in by a mounded, earthy ring of hills, as if the land had foreseen an invasion and thrown up a hasty bulwark. Against those defenses, the city flung tendrils of new development. Within them, it grew fatter, taller, denser.

Separated from Cincinnati by less than half a mile's worth of river, Covington's spacious streets were planned to line up precisely with their narrow and cratered cross-river counterparts. Standing now on Garrard Street, he could gaze across the river and see the mouth of Main, which ran Cincinnati's length, all the way up to Over the Rhine and the Liberties beyond. No pigs crowding these lanes, though, he noticed, working his way uphill from the riverbanks. No passed-out dockhands or bewildered foreigners blinking away the darkness of boats' bellies. Or maybe in Kentucky they just hid these things better than across the river.

If the streets here mirrored those in Cincinnati, the buildings did not. Ornate homes perched on hillocks of grass and garden. Iron fencing, topped with curlicued arrows, outlined each spacious plot. Here, he had heard, lived the coal barons amply feeding themselves by filling the burning mouths of the river's steamboats; the gentlemen farmers who traced their lineages back to the explorer Christopher Gist; the bachelor officers from the Newport barracks. Also here, hidden somewhere his recollection of Lafcadio's instructions refused to lead, was the widow of Delphebus Philip Walker IV, steamboat captain recently found facedown in the shallows of the river's northern shore, being, for the last time, pushed and pulled by the Ohio's current.

He finally found the house, brown and two-storied and imprisoned behind smooth, white pillars. The door sprung back like a trap after his third knock. It revealed a man's face that came to a sharp point, dulled by a patch of dark chin hair shot through with white. The man's smile lifted ears already stretched taut away from his face.

The man in the door looked him up and down. "You're Bosenbach."

He nodded.

The man grabbed his shoulder. "I'm Amos Shinkle. Lafcadio told you about me?"

"A little."

"A little is all Lafcadio knows."

Shinkle maintained a grip on his shoulder, guiding him down a narrow center hallway and into a plush sitting room.

"Here's your man experienced in these matters, Sophia," Shinkle said.

With her back to the men, the widow stood straight as a mast in front of a tall window, sectioned into squares. When she turned, his eyes went first to her face, a pale flare above the high neck of a black dress, and then to the child in her arms, no more than a few months old. She swayed and rocked and said nothing.

Shinkle said, "This Dutchman made a name for himself last year in the election troubles. Werner Bosenbach—you know of him, Sophia? Comes to cannon shooting, he's a huckleberry above a persimmon. Killed some Kentuckians, and they make him a hero."

"I am no hero." Werner had said this many times before. It always made him thirsty.

Shinkle, perched one leg over the other in an armchair, could not catch his laugh. Sophia's head jerked, and Shinkle's mirth melted into a cough. "He's humble, at least," Shinkle said. "What we need is not a hero. Tell us your knowledge of the ... situation."

Werner pictured Lafcadio, angled into a creaking chair at that Bucktown saloon two nights before, telling him: "The husband's dead. Fell offa his own boat, you believe that. Bright and shiny-new thing that is. Whole horde o' darkies jumpin' to the meter of his music. John Law over there reckons it an accident. Terrible tragiclike, but naught to be done. But the widow's convinced it's murder, and she's pointin' her finger all 'round, and like a good native-born she takes that pointin' finger right to the nearest what?—free and fairly elected official. Shinkle fella, city councilor, he is. Now he, like any good elected official what's faced with actual work, turns to an enterprisin' individual—my good self—for help. Friend would be stating it strong, sure, but I know him, he knows me. Right awaylike, your name comes to mind, so I say, sure, Boomin' Bosenbach's your man. But then I say—you'll appreciate this, Werner—then I say, but a man like that, an *investigator* like that, of his quality, isn't what you'd call a bargain. And he says, a bargain is not what we are looking for. Perfect, right?"

Wanting to tell Sophia that the dead stay with us, but her hollow stomach would someday fill, Werner looked at her and said, "I know your husband died."

Shinkle replied, "Tragical accident."

Sophia stopped moving, and the child writhed. "It was no accident."

"Dell guarded you from it," Shinkle said. "But the river business, it is dangerous." Shinkle turned to Werner. "Marshal Sturges assured me he found no evidence of murder."

"A marshal with opinions," Werner said. "A matter I have experience of."

Shinkle squinted at Werner. "I don't know any Dutch marshals, but in this part of the world, we show some respect to men that wager their lives to keep us safe."

"If he does his job at all, this make him finest marshal in the West."

Shinkle stood and tugged the bottom of his coat. "Sophia. This indulgence is over. You see this man can be of no possible use to us."

"I've not offered you anything." The widow's voice was low and steady. "Would you take a drink?"

Shinkle coughed. "It is Sunday. We know, of course, that God frowns on—" Cut short by Sophia's piercing stare, Shinkle sat down and busied himself adjusting waistcoat buttons. "We are, madam, in your home."

She turned again to Werner. “Mr. Bosenbach?”

“A whiskey, *ja, bitte.*” Werner had noticed the crystal bottles when he walked in. He hoped the liquor’s warmth would chase away the feathery murmur in his hands.

Sophia shifted the baby from her shoulder to the pit of her elbow and with the other hand lifted an etched decanter. “Mr. Shinkle is a temperance man, at least on Sundays,” she said, pouring a second glass. “Does God care for days of the week, do you think?” She walked a tumbler brimming with whiskey across the room to Werner and returned to the window, holding her glass in a tight fist. “Doesn’t He have bigger things to worry about?”

“*Prost.*” Werner poured half the shot down his throat.

Sophia swayed and bobbed like a buoy in a choppy swell, occasionally whispering to the baby, never spilling her whiskey. “Dell was raised on those boats. We were married on one. When his father died, that’s where he went. Not here. He didn’t slip and fall.” A cloud passed, and light from the window brought out the red around her eyes. She looked down at the child. “When he is grown, what he will have of us is stories. That story will not be that his father slipped and fell, and his mother ran back to Louisville. You will be paid two hundred and fifty dollars,” Sophia said, looking at Werner. “To find them.”

Werner raised his glass to her.

Shinkle protested, “Sophia–”

“Three hundred and fifty if you kill them.” Sophia gulped down her whiskey.

Shinkle stood. “Mrs. Walker!”

She turned back to the window, which provided a partially obscured view of the river’s southern turn away from Cincinnati. “We’re not much in Covington. The marshals are no help. 'Those people,' the marshal said. 'Those people that work the docks, they wind up dead sometimes.' And where else can I go? They all—" she waved a hand at Shinkle, "say the same thing." Sophia shook her head. She turned and pointed at Werner. "But you find them, and you kill them, and people will know. On this river, you don't just kill a Walker and leave him in the muck."

A silence followed, finally broken by Shinkle. "Yes, Bosenbach." At the sound of his voice, Sophia resumed her watch out the window. "Yes, we should like you to confirm or disconfirm the accidental nature of Mr. Walker's death."

"Where are you from?" Sophia said to the windowpanes.

A plain question, but in Werner's experience, one that led to accusations, insults, violence. "*Deutschland*, Bavaria."

"German. Or Dutch. People seem to use both."

"*Ja*. Same."

Shinkle, looking Werner in the eye for the first time since greeting him at the door, said, "You came here, to America, for this?"

"I don't hit a nail straight. I have worked the slaughterhouses in the winter, but in summer. ..." Werner shrugged. "There are only so many jobs in Cincinnati for Dutch."

"And yet so many Dutch in Cincinnati," Shinkle said.

Sophia turned to Werner and leaned forward, an aspen against a gale. "The men who killed my husband are out there. The law will do nothing—will you?"

Werner believed her. He wanted to believe her. He wanted her money. "I will find them."

The widow straightened and swallowed the last of her whiskey. "Good. That is good. He was on our new boat when he was—well, you can start there. The *High Water*. It's at the Landing." She turned back to the light pouring in through the window and dismissed the men with a wave. Werner and Shinkle left the room, through the house's door, out into a world bright and unleavened by anguish. Shinkle insisted on walking with Werner back to the ferry landing.

"There is certainty that grows from grief," Shinkle said. "Don't trust it." He gripped Werner's elbow as they awaited the ferry. "Lafcadio Murphy assured me you are the man to look into this and make of it quick work." When Werner did not respond, Shinkle added, "She needs peace, Bosenbach."

Werner managed to free his elbow and started down the riverbanks toward the boat that would take him back to Cincinnati.

2
The Rhine

Back across the river.

Through Bucktown and the Bottoms, blocks of bent and bowed wooden tenements heaped over saloons, past Dead Man's corner, where sometimes two nights would pass without a murder. North through the fourth, second, and fifth wards, and finally to the arched stone bridge spanning a narrow canal, which moved reluctantly in a precise line found nowhere in nature.

Back Over the Rhine.

Years before, with everything he knew buried under a receding horizon, Werner had seen the Rhine. He had crossed it on his way north from the village of Weichweiler. It was the most water he had ever seen before his seventy-three-day westward ocean voyage, folded into the dark and cramped *zwischendeck* on the ship *August Edward*. The Miami-Erie Canal that slipped through Cincinnati looked like that ancient river as much as a trembling tear resembles the heaving sea. But the brick tenements north of the canal filled with Bavarians, and the men singing in the *biergartens* were Württembergers, and the signs along Bremen Street read *Apotheke* and *Oeffentlicher Notar* and *Herrenfriseur*, so the canal became the Rhine, and the tenth ward above it was Over the Rhine. Werner had left Germany, but it had been here waiting for him.

Trailing the warm scent of reward and renewal laid on thick in letters from cousins and aunts, a steady rain of "Dutch" landed in Over the Rhine. Census takers found the population doubled every time they looked.

Werner had heard the stories. Over the Rhine: A bright, guffawing collection of city blocks that leaped and shouted *willkommen!* That taught Americans the meaning of *gemütlichkeit:* stein and *biergarten* brimming with lager and laughter, tenement matrons cheerfully mopping brick walkways, singing societies belting anthems of the Fatherland, and barmaids blowing at sweaty blond strands fallen across uncreased brows while carrying fistfuls of ceramic mugs, each as big as a man's thigh, to tables of laborers weary but not worn by honest work. Werner could find that Over the Rhine some weekends in the spring, on the Grammer's shaded and bustling patio, with the *wienerwurst* man telling him jokes, and a sufficient quantity of lager passing down his throat, but mostly he saw a people afraid to become different than they had been, surrounded by a sea of Americans scared by how different they were.

After the riots, and the cannon, it no longer mattered that he had not held a job longer than four months since arriving in Cincinnati three years before. Because people knew his name, they asked him to do things. After he met Lafcadio Murphy downtown, he mostly retrieved money people said they did not have. The name helped, so did his Colt Navy revolver with its stained handle. Recently, he hardly hit anyone.

Now a dead man's wife was looking into his eyes and asking for blood. Now he needed a drink. Over the Rhine bristled with saloons, dram shops, porter houses. On most days, and always on Sundays, the teetotalers gathered with their signs, warning of pestilence, of pauperism, of idiotic children. They yelled in English, as if volume added meaning to their words.

Werner usually enjoyed elbowing past the—invariably well-dressed and bathed—temperance protesters, but found he could not muster the enthusiasm. Instead he turned toward Heinrich's.

Heinrich, a bungmaker, took some of his proceeds in kind, and after a day of woodturning, opened his shop to anyone who could find the place and was willing to part with five cents for a mug of lager from whichever barrel he happened to have.

Otto was there, hunched toward a colossal stein as he was every other time Werner had gone in. Otto, who was seventy-three, but looked to Werner at least a hundred and ten, was brought to Cincinnati by a nephew. He refused to speak English, a language he considered effeminate. Werner nodded a greeting and took a stool next to the older man.

"*Die Kanone,*" Otto slurred. He brought his hands together before flinging them apart, fingers splayed. The explosion sound he made landed spittle on Werner's ear.

"*Ja, ja.*"

Otto lurched into song, unfurling a voice more enthusiastic than tuneful:

"*Gewissen hin, Gewissen her,*

Ich acht viel mehr die zeitlich Ehr,
Dien nicht um Glauben, dien um Gelt,
Gott geb, wie es geh in jener Welt."

Werner brushed some curled wood shavings from the table in front of him and looked at Heinrich, still wearing his work apron, sitting atop a cask of lager. Heinrich waited until Werner had placed a nickel on the table before he moved. He collected the nickel and frowned at Werner.

"I didn't bring it," Werner said.

Heinrich sighed through his nose and headed to the back room. He returned with a foggy glass that held spindle gouges and lathe chisels. These he dumped into a basket and held the glass up to Werner. Werner shrugged and Heinrich filled the glass from the barrel.

Werner drank down the lager, warm and tailed with sawdust. He slapped down another nickel. Then another, and another.

3
The Landing

The Public Landing was a wide, sloping pitch of hard, bare earth that receded into sucking mud at the city's southern edge. Boats—flatboats and rafts, too, but now mostly hulking and proud steamboats with gleaming sidewheels, or the older, cracked and listing rearwheelers—crowded the Landing, nosed in like hogs at a stinking trough.

Werner strode across the Landing looking for Walker's vessel among the dozens of steamboats stacked along the city's shore. He diverted his mind from the pain behind his eyes by cataloging the stores and offices that stood between the Landing and the rest of the city. Here they were, Cincinnati's clapboard teeth in a stained and crooked south-facing smile: Fred Shierberg's Groceries, Liquors, and Commission; the Bell & Brass Foundry; Rectified Whiskey; Irwin and Fisher, Commission Agents; Athearn and Hibberd, Commission and Forwarding Merchants and Steamboat

Agents, and so on for as far as Werner could see.

Werner said aloud, "Business," one of the only English words regularly used amidst the guttural German spoken Over the Rhine. He thought of Ignatz at the Turnverein telling him, "There are only two kinds of Americans: clergymen or soap salesmen." The Public Landing boasted no clergymen; the soap salesmen were everywhere.

Werner approached a huddling of roustabouts and asked for the *High Water.*

"Sure, Franz," said one, the biggest, "but it won't get you back to Dutch land."

One of the men, wearing a cap, slapped the big man's shoulder, smiling, but not getting a smile in return.

"No problem here," the big one responded. "Long as Franz ain't looking for work. 'Tween the niggers and the Irish it's—"

"Only looking for the *High Water.*" Werner felt his heart tapping at his shirt. "And it is *Deutschland.*"

"Dutch land, what I said."

"That's the *High Water* there," said the one in the cap, and he pointed to a steamboat whose gleaming white layers, decks, and rails looked to Werner like a cake waiting to be cut.

"*Danke.*" Werner angled down the landing, willing himself not to turn back, bracing for a blow that never came.

A teenager in a woolen black suit stood amid barrels and boxes on the *High Water's* forecastle, marking a sheaf of papers and sweating. Hearing Werner's footfalls on the gangplank, the boy spoke without looking up.

"She don't depart until next week. Not taking on any port passengers."

Werner continued up the gangplank. "Trouble is with

people leaving this ship, *ja?* Not boarding."

"She's a boat, not a ship." A reflex. Looking up now, and having heard Werner's accent, he enunciated slower and louder, "Not. Taking. Passengers."

Right in front of the boy now, Werner leaned left and right, taking in the boat from this new angle. "Very tall, this boat. If a man all the way up there fell ..." Werner traced an arc with his pointed finger from the top of the pilothouse—the boat's uppermost tier—to the lapping water below their feet. "... It would take a strong jump, *ja?* From up there, to clear all this decks."

Blushed with anger, the boy stammered, "You damned Dutch bastard—"

"*Ach.* My accent always starts me on the wrong hand. You say this, start on the wrong hand?"

"No, I don't say this," the boy spat. "It's foot."

"*Ja,* I have started on the wrong foot. Here is the right foot. I'm Werner Bosenbach. Mrs. Delphebus Walker gives me two hundred and fifty dollars to find her husband's killer. I will have a look."

With widened eyes, the besuited teen watched as Werner slipped past him onto the boat's main deck. Werner toed packages to determine their contents, gave the livestock a wide berth, and tried not to relive his own journey four years before from New Orleans, huddled on a main deck with three hundred others, this new world sounding much like the one he'd left behind.

As he had hoped, three men soon interrupted his half-hearted search: the one he bypassed on the forecastle, joined by an older, fuller man long used to the heat of a wool suit, and a tall, black man in shirtsleeves and a vest.

"There he is, Chief," said the boy.

"I am capable of discerning the man, Jesse," said the older counterpart, the gleam of authority in his eyes. "It is less clear to me how he was able to gain such unimpeded trespass to our main decks."

"I shoulda—"

"Never say 'I should have,' Jesse. It betrays a lack of conviction."

Jesse mostly managed to keep his chin from dropping. "Yessir."

The man turned to Werner. "It is customary to ask permission before boarding a vessel you do not command." He raised a hand to interrupt Werner's response. "But given that you are obviously a landman, and a Dutch to boot, we'll overlook it." The man exhaled, having addressed his first point, and looked again at Jesse. "Assistant Clerk, you say this man reported to you his business aboard the *High Water?*"

"Yessir. Told me Mrs. Walker give 'im two-hundred-fifty dollars to find who killed Captain Dell."

Turning back to Werner, "Is that a fact?"

"A fact."

The man examined Werner, starting at the muddied, worn boots, pausing at his holstered pistol, and ending at the rounded cloth hat preferred by the German immigrant.

"Difficult times for the Walker household. I am Chief Clerk Titian Ramsay Bliss, and that is Charles, our steward." He motioned toward the black man, who nodded. "You will join us on the boiler deck."

Moving out of the cargo area, the man stopped Jesse with a hand on his shoulder. "Assistant Clerk, a full inventory of the goods and cargo currently on board. In the future avoid giving the opportunity to rob us to any Dutch bastard that ambles up."

Werner followed Bliss, and was followed by Charles, into the darkness of a flight of interior stairs. They emerged into the sunlight on the second-level hurricane deck and passed through glass doors into a parlor illuminated by windows at the bow and stern and ornate lanterns along the walls. Ringed with cabin doors, the room spanned nearly the entire length of the boat and was filled uncomfortably with linened tables. When Werner stopped beneath a crystal chandelier and craned his neck, Charles sidestepped him and said, "Looks real, but it ain't. Just looks good." The men shuffled to a round table, set for ten with polished silver and gleaming china.

Bliss gestured with an open palm as he sat himself at the table. "Sit down, Mr. ... I apologize. Jesse told me the name you gave, but it escapes me."

It was Charles who answered, "Boomin' Werner Bosenbach." Turning to Werner, "The papers made you sound bigger."

"The papers, *ja.* All steamboats have this room?"

Bliss stared up at Charles.

"He stopped them riots last year, Chief," Charles said. "Up Over the Rhine, Know-Nothings going around smashing ballot boxes."

Bliss' face betrayed no recognition.

"There was a cannon?"

"Ah," Bliss grimaced. "Bad business all around. That was you, sir?"

Werner gave no response and catalogued the room's opulence. Liquor bottles polished to a high gloss behind a dark wood bar, a pair of elevated seats for shoe shining, all atop a plush carpet.

"This is our boiler deck parlor, Mr. Bosenbach," Bliss said, sweeping an arm around the space. "Here we have the dining facilities, the bar, the barber's room, and around it all ten passengers' cabins."

"Chief," Charles said, "we ain't selling him a cabin."

Werner examined the armory of silver laid out on the table in front of him and imagined all those glittering knives cutting through fat steaks on all those pristine plates. The chatter would be deafening. Coming up from New Orleans, when he was crowded on the main deck, he could not remember hearing it. "I took a steamboat in '52. I did not see this room."

"Truthfully, most of our passengers choose deck passage," said Bliss. "This room is a bauble, Mr. Bosenbach, a wand we wave around to attract rich passengers, who own much of the merchandise we tote from port to port. We spend as much on them as they spend on us. The deck, however, is where a boat sinks or soars."

Werner grunted and cast his eyes around the room again before focusing fully on the chief clerk.

"I suppose you'll be wanting to speak about Ray," Bliss said.

Werner watched Charles' hand solidify to a fist and his head snap at Bliss. The name meant nothing to Werner, but he knew a shut mouth usually brought more answers than any questions he could ask.

Bliss sighed. "He was aboard the *High Water* two days before they found Dell."

"Bixby Ray?" Charles said. "Bixby Ray was on this boat?" He waited for Bliss to respond, but the chief clerk stared impassively ahead.

Werner broke the tension. "Was this Ray a passenger?"

“This boat has not seen her first passenger. Just out of the graving dock a couple weeks ago,” Bliss replied.

“Then he is what?”

“Murdering bastard makes money outta grief, what he is,” Charles said. “Chief, this is how you tell me Bixby Ray was involved?”

“You can stow that attitude, Steward. I do not know that he *was* involved, and the day that I share with you every thought and figure in my head is a long way off.”

The two men glowered at each other. Reflected shards of light from polished silver danced across their faces.

Werner cleared his throat. “Not a passenger. Why does this Ray come to the boat?”

Bliss flicked his eyes toward Charles. “He came here in a ... professional capacity, looking to speak with Dell.”

“He comes here to kill and steal,” Charles said. “All legal, Fugitive Slave Act on his side.”

Werner leaned forward, ruining the carefully arranged landscape of cutlery with his elbows. “He would have reason to be here in professional capacity?”

“I only mark papers, tally sums, and sell cabins,” Bliss recited. “It does not matter if we did anything Ray believed us to have done. It matters that he believed it. He did.”

“Ray. You know where he is now?” Werner asked.

Bliss looked to Charles, who answered, “You ’a told me about this before, we’d know by now.”

Werner drummed his fingers on the soft linen. “I will find him.”

Charles leaned forward, pressing the table down with his palms. “Then what?”

Werner shrugged. “The widow pays extra one hundred for dead murderers.”

"Sophia." Bliss shook his head.

"You are both sure this man Ray does the killing?"

Charles' "Yes" was quick and firm.

Bliss looked at his lap.

Werner took in the room's trappings again. "Boiler parlor deck. How much is a cabin from New Orleans?"

Bliss said, "Twenty dollars. One way."

Werner exhaled a long whistle and looked up at Charles. "Looks good, though. Thank you for your help."

"That ain't the last of it," Charles said. "I'm coming with you."

"That is impossible," said Bliss. "A negro and a Dutch." He loosed a small laugh. "Like the punchline to some joke. You will find nothing but trouble."

Werner had thought much the same thing, but hearing it out of Bliss' mouth made it petty.

Charles slapped his palm against the table. "If you want to know where Ray is, we got to talk to the barber. You know him?"

Werner removed his cap and ran a hand through the greased, tangled mess. "I wear this beard and this cap so I don't have to pay a barber."

"Not a barber. *The* barber," Charles said and stood up from the table. "You come on, and bring that shooter of yours. You'll need it when we find Ray."

Werner looked at Bliss, whose face had soured into a grimace, then turned to Charles. "You know what this Ray looks like?"

"Couldn't forget his damned face if I tried."

"There will be no sharing of profit."

"I don't need your money, Boom. I got a job." Charles started for the door.

Bliss called after him, "That job needs doing."

Werner could see Charles roll his eyes. To the empty room ahead of him, Charles said, "Cabins all are squared away, Chief Clerk. Vittles are stored, and the liquor is on the shelf. I will be here, ready, and with that smile you like, by the time we supposed to shove off."

4
The Barber

Werner and Charles left the *High Water*, back into the day's sullen heat. Up the Landing, they neared the group of roustabouts that had given Werner directions, all jutted chins and squinted glares. The big one laced a viscous strap of tobacco juice across Werner's boot. A sharp laugh passed through the five men congregated around an overturned wagon.

"Mighty sorry, Franz," the big man said, drawing a hand across his messy grin. "Better have your boy clean that off."

A tight, toothless smile spread over Werner's face, bringing crags to his cheeks and a radiance of fine wrinkles around his eyes. He approached the man and said, "This looks like fine American tobacco on my boot."

Before he could respond, Werner kicked the inside of the roustabout's knee, eliciting a slippery pop from the joint. The big man, screaming, collapsed in the mud. Werner battered his howling mouth with the soiled boot, mixing blood and teeth and tobacco juice. He heard a thump on the ground behind him and turned to see Charles holding a small club over the prostrate figure of another roustabout. A knife lay by the roustabout's hand, open and limp. Bright blood leaked from his skull into the earth, darkening.

"We better go," said Charles. Already, turned backs had become staring faces.

Werner kicked the big man again in his broken, moaning mouth, then crouched to use the man's coat to clean his boot. Looking up at the other three men, Werner shrugged.

"Monday at the Landing, *ja?*"

When they had walked far enough away that they could no longer hear the moans, Charles turned to eye Werner, whose hands quaked at his sides.

"Nice for you, get to hit a man for calling you a name."

"You are always carrying that?" Werner nodded at the vest pocket that had swallowed Charles' club.

"I don't think 'a leaving that boat without a pistol in my belt and that blackjack in my pocket."

"You have a pistol? This man going to knife me, and you tap him over the head?"

Charles stopped walking and rounded on Werner. "Counting you, and I surely don't know as I can count you, but back there, counting you, I got one witness. If I'm gonna shoot some white man, I need *two* white witnesses say I was in the right, or I hang. Probably still hang if I had a gang 'a damn witnesses, but the law say I need two."

"You read newspapers and know the law. I have never met a negro like you."

"How many negroes you know?"

Werner shrugged. "I am thirsty."

Leaving the open plain of the Landing, Werner and Charles strode the dank closeness of Rat's Row, that stretch of Front Street between Vine and Walnut within smelling distance of the river. It was lined with saloons and shooting galleries, swallowing and spitting out customers day and night. They went east and turned onto Main. Werner followed Charles through the street crammed with river workers changing shifts, distrustful merchants overseeing the delivery of goods, émigrés staring upward at tenements, up to four stories high here and there, bigger than any they had seen since New Orleans.

In the face of a loose herd of trotting pigs, the men abandoned the cobblestones for the narrow sidewalk. The pocked swine marched in ignorant, litter-chewing bliss through the city streets, down to processing factories along the river where they were hit over the head with a hammer, torn apart, and emptied of their innards before being stuffed in barrels with a coating of salt and sent by boat to fill the empty breakfast plates of southern states.

Next to a furniture store on the corner of Fourth Street, a large glass pane carried the words "W. Watson, Barber" and surrendered a view of a single-chair operation with white tiled floors and a blotchy overhead mirror. Charles rapped a fist against the window and led Werner in.

The barber, a heavy black man in a white work coat grayed with sweat, paused before he leaped from his stool in the corner and addressed Werner. "A fine afternoon to you, sir. Come right in and take a seat."

Charles said, "Werner Bosenbach, this is—"

"Mr. Bosenbach," the barber interrupted, "your first

visit to me, am I correct? I remember my customers. Only have to tell me your liking once, and I've got it right up here." He tapped his graying temple. "What can I do for you today? A trim? A shave?"

Werner glanced over at Charles, who rolled his eyes toward the ceiling before turning to watch the street through the window.

"Perhaps a shave," Werner said, "just along the neck."

"Right you are. We'll stop that itching, and quick. Let that neck breathe in this heat."

Werner lowered himself into the reclining leather chair, and the barber unfurled a white frock. He snapped it at his side like he was taunting a bull and settled it on Werner's shoulders, covering him from neck to toe.

"A shave usually tallies at ten cent, but since you a new customer, let's make it eight."

"Charles told me—" It was Werner's turn to be interrupted.

"Charles told you about me?" The barber leveled at Charles a cold stare. "It's a fine friend makes referrals." He ran his straight razor over a strop in swift, jerking strokes. "A fine friend. 'Course, sometimes, that can bring more than you plan." He looked up from the razor in his hand to meet Werner's eyes in the mirror, flashed a luminous smile. "Not the case today, though, as you can see. I'm as free as if Moses himself had led me to this very spot." The barber lathered his brush in a wooden soap bowl.

Charles turned from the window. "Bill, he's all right. We need to talk about Bixby—"

"You know why I don't cut colored hair, Mr. Bosenbach?"

The barber painted Werner's throat with thick, warm

lather. Werner could see only the ceiling. He swallowed quickly as the brush crossed his Adam's apple, and the barber answered his own question.

"Plenty of reasons, really. Not *you* now, you clearly a forward-thinking man, but plenty of my customers, they all white folks, they wouldn't much like the idea of sitting in the same chair held a colored man's posterior. His behind, y'understand. Not one bit. They'd love that like the Devil loves holy water. Wouldn't much like neither looking down at the ground and seeing their fine, upstanding hairs mixing with our curly, nasty ones. Sure, must be something in the Bible against that." The barber raised his head to find Charles in the mirror. "But mostly, it's 'cause negroes talk too damn much."

Werner drew in a quick breath as he felt the razor blade touch his throat.

"But you know what I mean, knowing Charles." The barber's tone had regained its entrepreneurial brightness. The razor's strokes were quick and light.

"I meet Charles only today," Werner said.

"Only today! And already, he's directing you to Cincinnati's finest barber. A fast friend. A fast friend, indeed." Having completed the first pass on Werner's neck, the barber applied another layer of thick, warm lather. "What is it you do, Mr. Bosenbach? Seems to me I've heard that name before."

"Lafcadio Murphy says I am *investigator.*"

"Charles *and* Lafcadio Murphy. You do keep an invigorating social circle, if you don't mind my saying, sir."

"*Ja.*" Werner quickly swallowed a laugh, feeling the blade against his throat.

"And what is it you investigate, sir?"

"I am right now finding man who killed Delphebus Walker the Fourth. Steamboat captain. Charles worked for him."

"I ain't arguing, but right now, you ain't doing that. Right now, you receiving the finest shave a man can buy in the West. And at less than face value." The barber pulled Werner's skin taut and scratched the blade steadily across his neck. "That's some barber humor for you, now. Face value." The barber grinned. "The fourth, huh? He some kinda prince?"

"Kind of prince works the river," Werner replied.

"And who would kill a prince like that?"

"We hoped you could tell us."

The barber lifted the blade from Werner's throat and stepped back. "Me? You seen my name on the window. Says, W. Watson, Barber. If he ain't opening a barbershop next door, I wouldn't've killed him." He ducked his head back toward Werner's neck. "He opening a shop next door?"

Werner shook his head minutely. "We look for man named Bixby Ray. A slave hunter."

"You reckon this Ray killed that captain?"

Werner's shoulders rose in a shrug. "Bad men do bad things."

The barber paused at his work and stood erect, pointing the straight razor at Werner's chest. "All kinds of men do bad things." He bent over again, applying quick, short strokes to Werner's throat. "And if you find him?"

"The captain's widow pays extra for killing."

The barber stepped back to assess Werner's now bare neck. "Sounds like dangerous work."

"*Ja,* can be. If you are not prepared."

The barber lifted a corner of Werner's smock to wipe

away a dollop of shaving foam and revealed Werner's right hand gripping his revolver, cocked and pointed at the barber.

"Werner, put that down!" Charles started from the window. "Bill, I didn't—"

"You stay right there, boy." The barber pointed at Charles but held eyes with Werner. "See what you brung me?"

"Do you know the location of Bixby Ray?" Werner asked the barber.

"And if you find him, you kill him?"

Werner shrugged.

The barber turned to Charles. "Don't take a damn thing to kill. I seen that back in Maryland. Ignorant, unreading men don't know nothing about nothing, they some of the best killers going."

"It takes something to kill," Werner said. *It keeps taking,* he thought and glanced at the stain on his gun handle. Quicker than Werner imagined the man capable, the barber moved, and Werner felt the thin edge of the razor against his neck.

"Just a flick, that's all it takes," the barber said quietly. "Now, let's you put up your gun and me lower this blade, and we get back to talking."

"*Ja,*" Werner whispered. "Let's." He slid the revolver back to its holster and held his breath.

The barber lowered his razor and looked at Charles. "Can't happen. Can't kill no slave hunters in these streets." He jerked his head at Werner. "Even if you get this fool to do the shooting, who will they blame? Bucktown will burn. '41 again—damn it, Charles, you old enough to remember that shit. You interested in taking this man places, take him down to the bakery on Fifth they burnt down, or the book store on Main, what's left of it. Take him down the first ward and show him where the militia stood by and watched those boys burn up our houses. Then take him up to the jail where they put us while the mob still in our streets." The barber walked to the window, watched pedestrians passing. "The only way we get to live is if we're the peaceable community. That means no spitting in the street. No gambling. No drinking that mess. It means turning the other cheek. And if we can do that, then in the night, some nights, we can do some good." The barber walked back to the chair and tore the frock from Werner's chest. He lifted it and snapped it down forcefully. He hung it on a hook and looked at Charles. "This town gets savage as a meat ax. Too many folks at risk, Charles, you know that. If this your damn fool way of asking, you made a poor fist of it. The answer is no."

The barber turned his back on Charles and Werner and wiped the razor with a clean rag.

"He was there in January," Charles said.

The barber's pistoning elbows froze.

"He was there," Charles repeated.

The barber pointed at the reflection of Charles' face in the mirror. "Don't give me no gum, boy."

"He was there."

The barber leaned on the basin in front of him. He spat and shook his head. "Don't matter. He ain't the biggest toad in this puddle. We're doing something here, Charles, something bigger than either of us, bigger than your Captain Delphebus Walker the Fourth." His voice lowered to a hoarse whisper. "Bigger than them Garners." He turned back to Werner. "And you, sir, I believe I'll have to charge you the full ten cent."

5
The President

"Close shave," Werner said, hand to his own throat. "A drink?"

"We don't have time for no drink, Boom."

"There is always time for a drink."

Already moving west, Charles said over his shoulder, "When your daddy told you not to do something, what did you do next?"

Werner took a few long strides to catch up. "When my father told me not to? I was hit. Then he died. I was not hit so often then."

Charles cast his eyes at Werner's face to find it unmarred by this memory. "Shit, Boom, that's not what I meant. You go talk to your mother, get her permission, right?"

"I never did this. You would do this?"

"Well, no. It's just something—I never met my daddy." Charles smeared sweat across his brow with the back of his forearm. "The point is, we're going to see the president."

"Pierce?"

"No, Boom."

Werner smiled. "*Ja*, fine. This man will know where Ray is?"

"Might be."

"Will he have lager?"

"They's Quakers, so I'd guess not."

"Quakers."

By the time they made it to Sixth and Elm, half a mile west of Watson's barbershop, they had left behind the herds —people and pig. The heat thickened, reaching a late afternoon peak. One knock, and the door opened like Charles had hit it with both barrels of a shotgun.

Out jutted an enormous beak nose in the middle of a face that looked like a waxen death mask held too close to a flame. The chin's considerable weight melted away from the crown, leaving the whole face lengthened and narrowed. Deep, wishbone-shaped grooves ran from his nostrils to the sides of a conspicuous jaw that opened with, "Thou shalt have refuge!"

From beneath the stubbled jaw, the man's claws flailed wildly, grasping at Charles. The jaw turned, exposing an unkempt cascade of whitened, loose hair, thin at the top and shaggy by the ears, and opened in a shout.

"Catherine!"

Charles, a step removed from the man's hands, still shooting out like eels disturbed from dark sleep, said, "Mr. Coffin!"

From inside, "Levi! Levi! Await me!"

Through the half-opened door, Coffin aimed his chin once more at the men outside.

"Mr. Coffin," Charles said, "we don't need no refuge today."

Charles saw Coffin's jaw make an inward turn, while his hands reached out again. "Catherine!"

"Mr. Coffin! It's Charles. We've met. With Bill Watson? We just need to converse with you a moment."

Werner, a few steps back, eyed the street for neighbors or passersby curious about the racket. Coffin let the door open fully, revealing a wiry frame that did not seem up to the task of hauling around its outlandish head. Behind Coffin's arm against the doorframe, his wife perched, catching her breath from the short sprint to the door. She took in the chaotic scene with calm eyes.

"To converse?" Coffin said. "Words are dust in the eyes of the Lord, boy. It's action we need."

Werner leaned forward over Charles' shoulder. "*Ja,* this is what we hope to converse. Action."

"Let them in, Levi," said the woman.

"In with thou both. In! Before the enemies of liberty descend." Coffin pointed behind him through the entry, keeping his jittering eyes on the street until the door slammed shut, and he latched no fewer than three bolts across its frame. He led the men into a cramped sitting room where Coffin started in as if the visitors had interrupted him mid-tirade. "Bill Watson is forever holding forth on that John Rankin. It's up in Ripley, this, and Uncle John that. As if the man invented the underground. Is John Rankin known to slaves and slave hunters alike as the President of the Underground Railroad?"

Coffin was up and pacing, pointing an occasional finger to the ceiling. His wife took the brief opportunity of his turned back to introduce herself as Mrs. Coffin. Except for the tight bonnet fastened over her wrinkled head, Werner thought she looked exactly like her husband.

"No, he is not!" Coffin said. "As a preacher, he's a bust, and no better is he as a farmer. Lights a candle on top of that hill of his, and he is the savior of all negroes? What does he know of it? It tries a man's soul to be an abolitionist, Chauncey. Brickbats, stones, and rotten eggs are some of the arguments we meet. But as the poet says, 'Thrice is he armed who hath his quarrel just.'" Coffin beamed and waggled his eyebrows at Charles. "Now, one could rightly say mine own business is not flourishing, but I was riding slaves out of Carolina before Rankin could tell a runaway from a rutabaga. Have I told thou, Chauncey? The time I rode that slave out of North Carolina, a hunter in our midst?"

"Yes sir, Mr.—" Charles said.

Coffin continued, unabated. "It was my uncle Bethuel had the slave, in point of fact. Mine was a more dangerous role. Speed and subterfuge were my allies that day."

"Oh, Levi," said Mrs. Coffin with a smile, not looking up from her cross-stitch.

"I was just a boy of twenty-three, and Bethuel had set off in the wagon with a fugitive named Jack. He'd been made free by his owner, only to have the owner die and his poxy son proclaim this man slave again. Well, Bethuel has him in the wagon, headed for Pennsylvania—some Friends up there agreed to take the man in and give him work—and we get word that Osborne—a spiteful and low farmer scorned by all who met him—he's after them, as he thinks Bethuel's got his own runaway, named Sam if I remember correctly. Of course, Bethuel doesn't have Sam. Sam's secreted away in the thicket behind our house. But Osborne's heard that Bethuel's traveling with a colored companion, and he's sure it's his Sam."

Werner was having a hard time keeping up with the pace of Coffin's speech. Caught on the meaning of one word, he missed whole sentences. He kept his face blank and tried to fathom the purpose of this story, this visit, this house, this land.

Coffin continued, "Cousin Vestal looks upon me and says, 'Levi, take Elkanah.' That was our fastest horse. 'Levi, take Elkanah, and get up that trail to Bethuel.' I was meant to warn Bethuel, and mayhaps to hide the fugitive. That was left to me. But on my way, who should I meet but Osborne, the man himself."

"Levi, the distance, dear," said Mrs. Coffin softly.

Coffin's dark eyes snapped down from their storytelling reverie, and he spun to glare at his wife, who continued her stitching, willfully unaware of her husband's silent rebuke. "As I was about to mention," Coffin said, "by the time I had come upon Osborne, I had passed by some distance that small elm tree which marked the furthest I had previously traveled from home. I crossed the Dan River ford, and beyond that, all was new and strange to mine eyes. Even without all that followed, it would have been a wondrous adventure!"

"*Ja,* wondrous," Werner said, an attempted dam in the flood of Coffin's words. "If I—"

"Wondrous! Yes, but I had just found Osborne, angry and full of drink." Werner's dam just a smooth stone over which Coffin's story flowed undisturbed. "Coming upon the hunter before finding his prey, I was all excitement. I deceived the man," Coffin flashed an impish grin that was pushed back to solemnity by his jaw, "but told no untruth."

Mrs. Coffin nodded. "Told no untruth."

"Traveling to see a cousin, I told him, and in his excitement, he enrolled me in finding his runaway."

"And when you came upon Bethuel, Osborne saw the fugitive was not his slave and was convinced to go home," Charles said hurriedly. "Our business is—"

"We soon came upon Bethuel and his wagon," Coffin said. "He, traveling blindly unaware of the dangers behind him, was turned around mightily by my arrival with Osborne. But luckily for us all, he gave away nothing. I introduced the men, and discerning that Osborne did not recognize Jack, despite a hundred-dollar reward for him advertised in the papers, made a show of allowing Osborne to inspect to his heart's content. He admitted Bethuel did not carry the negro he was after, and agreed to turn home. I turned with him and bade Bethuel and Jack a safe journey, which they had. Of the two thousand or more slaves I have personally shepherded to freedom, that was the first." Coffin sighed, his upright pose and lifted chin relaxing into a more natural posture. He smiled and nodded at Charles. "I have Nantucket blood flowing in these arms, Chauncey. I cannot be denied!"

"A great help you've been to your fellow man, Mr. Coffin. That's why we here today."

Coffin's brows rose. "Does someone need refuge? We stand ready! Do we not stand ready, Catherine?"

"Of course, Levi," Mrs. Coffin's attention still firmly on her stitching. "I cleaned out the hidey holes just yesterday."

"No, Mr. Coffin, Mrs. Coffin, thank you," Charles said. "It's information we're after. There is a slave hunter named Ray."

"Slave hunters! Where do you think they stop first when they visit Cincinnati?" Coffin shook his head. "Insolent and corrupt souls. They tax my patience."

"And the mud they bring in every time they enter the house," added Mrs. Coffin.

Werner looked down at his own crusted boots.

"Uninvited." Mrs. Coffin crinkled a smile at Werner.

"It is many a stockholder who fears these men, who would come and snatch freedom away from the negro. Most of our passengers nearly as white as you and I." Coffin nodded at Werner with widened eyes.

"We look for this slave hunter, Bixby Ray. You have heard this name?" Werner looked back and forth from Coffin's face to his wife's brow, tilted over her handiwork.

Coffin rocked back his head, leveraging his nose upward. "I believe I *have* heard this name. He is a slave hunter?"

"*Ja.*"

"And he has stolen a great many fugitives back into captivity?"

"Yes," said Charles.

"He that stealeth a man and selleth him, he shall surely be put to death!"

"That is the plan," Charles said.

"That is *Exodus,*" said Coffin. "And verily, I say unto this Ray, though he be not present, inasmuch as thou hast done it unto the least of these my brethren, thou hast done it to me!"

"That's lovely, Levi," said Mrs. Coffin.

"*Ja,* lovely," added Werner. "Do you know where he can be found?"

"I will accept nothing less than a bill of sale from God Himself as proof of one man's ownership of another!" Coffin declared. "And when the dictates of humanity come in opposition to the law of the land, we ignore the law!"

Werner, chin dipped and eyebrows raised, looked at Charles.

"Mr. Coffin," Charles said, "we was thinking that given your position—"

"President of the Underground Railroad. Yes, they do call me that. I did not give it to myself, Chauncey, but it is a burden I will carry." Coffin shot up from the seat he had just taken. "Thou wilt see this and weep!"

He swept out of the room, and soon Werner heard his clomping feet ascending to the home's second and third floors. Mrs. Coffin lowered her stitching to her lap. Werner smiled indulgently at her, but her face was cold and still.

"Stockholders. Passengers. Depots and lines. He is like a child at play." She massaged fingers crooked from sewing. "When he comes back, he'll tell you the story of Jane. It is not a bad one, and shorter than most. Do not ask of him any questions if you care to leave this home before nightfall." Mrs. Coffin seemed to straighten and grow with each word. She turned to Charles. "You brought this matter to Mr. Watson?"

Charles answered by examining the floor between his feet.

"And he told you, sensibly, that killing this slave hunter will solve nothing? That it will, in fact, cause far more damage than you imagine? So, you came here, to this home, with this man who is unknown to us," she tilted her bonnet at Werner, "and wished for different answers. You will not find them."

Werner felt the need to defend himself but could not find the words. He found that his shoulders had shrunk forward. He looked back toward the door. If he'd been able to find a drink before they entered, he would know what to do now. Charles lifted his head to meet Mrs. Coffin's steady gaze. Werner saw in his eyes wet anger and frustration.

"He was there," Charles said. "This Ray, in January. The Garners."

Mrs. Coffin deflated visibly into her chair and looked away, a hand to her mouth. The only sound in the room was muffled thuds of Coffin wandering the upper floors. Mrs. Coffin adjusted her dress and spoke to the wall. "You are certain."

"I saw him."

She turned and pinned Charles to his chair with her austerity. They could hear Coffin excitedly bounding down the stairs, and she said, "You will go to Dr. Maleachi on Vine and Seventh. You will tell him that Mrs. Coffin desires a tincture to help her cough. He will tell you where to find this slave hunter."

The thuds of her husband were approaching the main floor landing.

"Slave hunters are all devils, and it is no harm to kill the devil," Mrs. Coffin said. She looked at Werner, then at Charles and gave a firm nod.

"Yes, ma'am," said Charles.

Mrs. Coffin picked up her stitching and reapplied her placid smile as Coffin tumbled into the room. "Good then," she said, all treacly warmth.

"Ah!" Mr. Coffin shouted. "I must tell you about Jane!"

6
The Slave Hunter

At the confluence of Vine Street and Seventh, where the flooding waters of the Ohio occasionally deposited a great fan of silt when the untamable river spit its bit and ran for the hills, hung a long wooden sign, swinging below an iron railing. Against a blood-red background, it displayed the painted likeness of a man whose squinted eyes and upturned chin sought out the future, whose hands clutched at hips above fringed hunting trousers that fell to the beaded tops of furred moccasins. "Habakkuk Maleachi," the sign read. "Indian Doctor offering medical services to the suffering world of Cincinnati."

Through the front window, Werner parsed the tangle of items in the display: Dried and molded stingrays held aloft by twine swung idly past plaster molds of various dismembered limbs and heads, colored and etched to show the doctor's familiarity with the insides of bodies. Dried flowers dropped crusted petals on shelves crowded with talismans, and murky, yellow-tinted jars roiled with snakes, toads, and animals Werner could only guess at. A framed sign that perched next to these bottles of remains announced the presence on Thursday nights of "The Magnetic Doctress Miss Tennessee Claflin, Teller and Seer of Fortune(s)."

Inside, Werner recognized Dr. Maleachi right away. He stood behind a wooden counter, striking the same pose as on his sign. His tanned skin was sagged by age, and he was straight as a planed board. Like predatory animals in hiding, his eyes followed the men furtively from the caves under his brow.

A parrot, perched in a cage by the door, shook its head as Charles and Werner passed. "Ca! Ca! Coon!" it screeched. "Niglet! Errah! Niglet!"

A pebble flew at its cage, pinging among the iron bars. Werner, who had been staring at the bird, turned to see Dr. Maleachi's hand return to his hip.

Charles glared at the parrot, and asked over his shoulder, "Did that bird just call me a niglet?"

Dr. Maleachi inhaled deeply. "Its previous owner imparted ... *unfortunate* habits."

As though confessing under torture, the parrot screamed, "Coon! Coon!" Maleachi loosed another pebble, and the bird busied itself scratching its neck with a taloned foot.

"Better to keep bird quiet," Werner said.

"It is not in the nature of this beast to speak," Maleachi said. "Or to hate, but we have made it do both. You blame the bird?"

"I heard worse," Charles said. He turned away from the parrot, shaking his head. "We're here for Aunt Cathy's tincture."

Maleachi's hooded eyes took another pass over the two men in his store, then he gestured for them to follow him through a cloth-covered doorway into a cramped back room. He folded his arms and hunched, the posture of a tall man in close quarters. Only when Charles asked him directly about the slave hunter did Dr. Maleachi draw himself up, cast his gaze down at them along the sharp angle of his nose, and intone, "St. James Saloon."

"The Old Stump," Werner said. "It is where we should have started."

Maleachi seemed disappointed. "You know it?" He quickly regained his composure, speaking in a deep register and looking out through half-closed eyelids. "You will require spiritual protection for this journey. A divine tincture—"

"*Danke*, Doctor, but this is all the protection my spirit needs." Werner drew his pistol.

Maleachi stiffened, scraping the ceiling with the crown of his head.

"Damn, Boom." Charles said. "You can't keep that thing holstered for a whole hour at a time? Man helps us—buy something from him."

Driving the gun back into its sheath, Werner shrugged and tried to locate something in the room he could name. Amber bottles furry with dust sat in lines along two shelves behind Maleachi. From the low ceiling dangled wiry dream catchers and twirling feathers, long as Werner's forearm. Maleachi assumed a crossed-arm slouch. Werner gestured to the bottles.

"What have you got with whiskey in it?"

Maleachi groaned. "It all has whiskey in it."

Werner finished the last of the "Fortified Tincture, Guaranteed to Lift Spirits and Banish Vapors" by the corner of Fourth. He left the bottle in pieces on the cobblestone. "That," Werner belched, "was terrible."

"You didn't have to drink it all down," Charles said, as they headed south to Rat's Row.

Werner cocked his head at him, frowned, said nothing.

An oil-black crow waddled toward them, screeching and jabbing the air with its beak. It pecked and cawed, taunting them with open wings as if it could push them back the way they came. Werner bent swiftly at the knees, feinting a jump at the bird, which turned and, rocking on widened claws, delivered a final insult by not bothering to take flight. Charles and Werner followed the bird the length of a block, and when it hopped up a couple wooden steps and slipped in the open door of the St. James, Werner stepped in after it.

Inside, the crow rattled its claws atop a curving bar, snacking at something in the bartender's hand. He, along with the bar's forty or so now-silent patrons, stared at Werner and Charles.

"You don't look like coppers," the bartender said.

Werner scratched his cheek and smiled at the crowd and then at the bartender. "We are not."

The bartender nodded down at the bird. "Wally only runs in here if the coppers are coming. You sure?"

"Hear me speak. I am Dutch." He pointed to Charles. "Look at his face. You need a new watchman."

A crack erupted into the quiet that made Werner flinch. The billiards player smirked, and with that signal the saloon returned to a commotion of indistinct conversation.

The bartender clicked his tongue at the bird. "Wally's no good with colors, are you, love?" He tickled the massive bird beneath its imposing beak. "No surprise, black as he is." It leaped off the bar and trudged outside.

Werner drummed his fingers on the bar top. "A lager for me. Charles?"

Charles gave a firm shake of his head.

"A lager for me and a whiskey for my friend," Werner said.

While the drinks were poured, Werner surveyed the saloon, filled at this early afternoon hour with roustabouts and clerks, river workers of all kinds bringing their meager pay to the closest place that would take it, surrounded by done-up women and gamblers hoping to oblige them.

They found an unoccupied table, and Werner drained half his beer in the first sip. "*Ach*, terrible!" He smiled. "But a day with bad lager, it is brighter than without, *ja?*" He tilted the whiskey down, tumbling after the lager.

Charles replied to the space over Werner's shoulder, "I don't see him here."

"He will be. I trust that Mrs. Coffin." Werner jerked his head back toward the bar. "At least this one doesn't yell at you."

Charles stopped searching the bar. "What?"

"This bird, does not care you are a negro."

Charles shook his head. "If that's true, he's the only one."

Werner took another long slurp of lager.

"You keep drinking like that, you won't have legs to catch Ray."

"Drinking! This is lager, Charles. Dr. Just Walcker takes five gallons a day. It keeps him going."

“Keeps him going to the saloon.”

Werner raised his glass. “Safer five times than water. And ten times as savory.”

Sitting in silence, surrounded by noise, Werner closed his eyes and saw rolling Bavarian hills and whitewashed cottages framed in dark wood.

“He’s here,” Charles said.

Werner opened his eyes to Cincinnati. “The slave hunter?”

Charles sat back in his chair, letting its creaks and groans answer.

Werner drained down the last of his lager and sucked the froth from his mustache. “Where?”

Charles nodded to a shadowed corner where a man stood at the bar’s end, speaking to three levee hands who stared into their drinks.

Werner pushed his chair away from the table and felt the beer’s flush in his face. He walked crookedly to the group of men, hooked his thumbs in the pockets of his coat, and waited for the men to turn his way. When they did not, he interrupted, “You are Bixby Ray, the slave hunter.” The smile did not leave Ray’s face, but Werner saw his hand draw closer to his belt.

“I am Bixby Ray. I git things that run off. People’s property. Who are you?”

“Werner Bosenbach.”

The three dock workers wordlessly stood, picked up their drinks, and shuffled to the furthest corner of the bar.

Ray watched them cross the room, then squinted at Werner. “My new friends seem to think you’re bad company. You bad company?” Ray’s hand stroked his pistol.

Werner could make out a derringer in his waistcoat

pocket. He could also see that while Ray was drawing Werner's eye to the gun, the slave hunter's other hand was slipping into a coat pocket for a blackjack or a knife. "*Ja*, to some," Werner said, and drew back the hem of his coat, displaying the dark, stained handle of his own revolver.

The bartender took one tentative step toward them, thought better of it, and found a distant glass in need of polishing.

"I was in the middle of a story so good it'd punch your teeth out," Ray said.

"I would hear it if you don't mind drinking with a damned Dutch."

"Damned Dutch?" Ray shook his head. "I'll tell you this, friend—this may be the north, but it's still America, and one man don't need feel lower than any other. We fought for that back in '76." He smirked at Werner. "Long as you ain't Quaker."

"Catholic."

Ray stared at Werner, jabbed a finger in his chest, then slapped his hands on the bar, leaving his weapons undrawn. "A vhisky for the Papist Verner! Good then. I was just telling those boys about the damnedest nigger."

Werner sipped at the whiskey that Ray gulped down. By Ray's third, Werner had come to the bottom of his first.

"This boy, I'm telling you, he had us flummoxed. Flummoxed and bamboozled. How in a right world do a nigger with no legs not only escape from the plantation—where, believe me, they keep a good eye—but then make it across damn near the whole South, too? Usually, Werner, they stick close to home, which, why leave in the first place? Food and drink given to 'em. Better'n what I get at home, I'll tell you that." Ray's glassed eyes searched Werner for some reaction, and seeing none, rolled up to find the string of his story floating away. "What was I on about?"

"A negro with no legs escaped," Werner said.

Ray lifted his pointer finger and jabbed it at Werner three times. "That's it! It's times like these they get to callin' on me to set things back right. These fellas with the slaves, they ain't used to any work like that. That there's the point, right? So, I'm out there with the dogs, a-running 'em into the ground and a-hollerin', trying to find this boy. It'd be fun, if'n it wasn't so damned hot. What was his name? Damn. Didn't have no place out in them woods. Plenty 'a times I thought we had the trail, the dogs' tails up and waggin', I'm sure just around that next bend, we'd see that boy dragging his ass up north." Ray snorted and tilted back another whiskey. "North! Ha. Up 'ere they like talking about free and equal without thinkin' it through much. Was a time, I could make a trip to Pennsylvania and come back flush, but now? Shit, you might as well look for a needle in a haystack as for a nigger among Quakers." Ray brayed and slammed his glass against the bar. "So, I have to come out here, and I see how it is." Ray swiveled around to face the three levee hands, still huddled around their corner table. "Any of you specimens of northern manliness have something to say to ol' Werner? Something about his church or his funny accent?"

The levee hands were quiet.

Ray folded forward and grasped at his rifle, which leaned against the bar next to him. "When my business here is done, Werner, I'm back home to Virginia, where men *are* free and equal."

As he lifted the rifle, the three men bolted through the door, leaving a column of sunlight filled with falling sawdust swirling in the eddies of the draft. Ray brought the rifle to his shoulder, and Werner lifted it by its stock out of Ray's sweaty hands. Ray stared at the open door, his empty hands raised as if still holding the rifle, as two black men passed by. They didn't hazard a glance into the saloon from which three men had just exploded.

"They're just walking around, careless as you like, with no one. It's dangerous, Werner. Dangerous."

Werner leaned the rifle back against the bar, and slurped at his glass, beading in the heat. "What happened to that runaway?"

Ray narrowed his eyes at Werner. He looked ready to swing a fist before he broke into a sloppy grin. "Oh, that damned boy, couldn't find him for an age. Would you believe that? Downright embarrassing is what that is. You work years, folks know you for a thing, then something like, damn! George. That was his name, George. Werner, something like him comes along and now you just a man can't track a legless nigger." Ray swayed toward Werner and bobbed his head in a parabola of drunkenness. "I'll tell you Werner, the way I reckon it, it was the trees." He swayed back. "Yessir. Like back in Africa, George swung his way North limb to limb, like a little ol' scared monkey running from the lions." Ray chuckled to himself.

"Southern negroes do this, swing in the trees?" Werner asked, staring into his whiskey.

Ray burst out laughing, slapping his knees. But his face dropped and then hardened as he eyed Charles approaching them from his table. "All the time, Werner."

7
The Law

"What was you, listening him to death?"

With Ray's limp body between them, Werner and Charles stumbled down the cobbled street. The slave hunter's sweaty head lolled irregularly, forcing Werner and Charles to crane their necks back and forth to see each other.

"I was investigating." Werner smiled.

"You heard him about blacks swinging in trees. That ain't for fun, Boom. Let's open his throat right here."

Werner did not answer. He thought about the whiskey left in his glass back at the saloon.

Charles stopped walking, bringing them to a halt. "I'm serious. It won't get easier than right now."

"*Scheisse.*" Werner released his side of the slave hunter, who reflexively clung to Charles before sliding to the ground. Getting dark out by now, plenty of folks around, but none who cared. Ray was not the first drunk to fall face down on Sixth Street.

"Charles, we talk to this man. See what he says. If he killed Captain Walker, *wunderbar*, we take him to Mrs. Walker. And if accident happens on the way—well, it is a dangerous river. I split the extra hundred with you. Right now, on this street? *Nein.* That entire saloon watched us drag this man out. If we kill him now, who will they blame?"

Charles, hands on his hips, turned to survey the street, mountainous shadows and smoking lanterns. "All right. I know a place." The place Charles knew was a closed door next to shuttered windows three blocks east on Front Street. Charles pounded twice with his free hand, added a softer knock, and said, "Maggie Spurlock!"

The sound of unlatching locks was followed by the scrape of the door's hinges as it swung outward. A woman in petticoats and a purple satin dress stood in front of a curtain that blocked from view the room behind her. Her decorous smile disintegrated into a scowl when she absorbed the three-man tableau. "Shit, Charles."

"I know," Charles said. "We need one of your rooms."

"Who's this?" she asked, jutting her chin at Werner. "And who the hell is all that?" She waved a hand at Ray who still sagged between them.

Charles jerked his head. "Over there, that's Boomin' Werner Bosenbach."

Werner rolled his eyes and smiled wanly. She showed no sign of recognizing the name.

"And this a man I hit over the head. Please. We need a place."

The woman looked over their shoulders across the street, watching a group of top-hatted men pass. The men spoke in low voices, looking back when they reached the corner. Through the curtain behind her came a muffled but insistent stomping rhythm.

She moved closer to Charles and hissed, "Why you bringing me this trouble? Here?"

"Goddamn. Boom, take this." Charles dropped his shoulder, passing the slave hunter's full weight to Werner, and walked with the woman a few paces down the street.

Werner stood, wreathed in Ray's stench, staggering a little under the weight. A tightening burn spread through his lower back. He could not make out Charles' hurried clumps of words nor the woman's replies, but when Charles pointed at him, and the woman glanced back, Werner grimaced a smile at her. In his arms, Ray gurgled and drooled. Charles turned back to the woman, who flattened the front of her dress, raised her chin, and returned to the door.

"You all can have a room. Costs five dollars."

Shifting Ray further around onto his back, Werner's head snapped up. "Charles!"

"I wanted to leave him on the street, Boom. This or that."

"*Scheisse.* Business. *Ja*, five dollars."

She parted the curtain behind the door and held it open to allow Charles and Werner, connected again by the unconscious slave hunter, to pass through into a stifling parlor filled with a murmuring crowd. Oily smoke from the gas lamps mixed with belches of tobacco and wafts of redolent perfume. An ornate wooden bar, backed by shelves filled with liquor, dominated one side. An archway through the other side revealed a tangled and tripping mass, a pulsating ring of dancers keeping time with the blast of banjo, viol, and fiddle, adding rhythms with pounding feet, slapped hands and thighs. Taking in the room, Werner realized the unconscious slave hunter and he were the only white men present. Feeling faces turn in their direction, he suppressed a strong desire to drop Ray and make some apology. Instead, he followed the woman, as best he could, across the parlor and up a set of stairs.

On the second floor, the woman spoke to the empty hallway ahead of them. "You lucky. We don't normally have rooms to spare."

Werner whispered to Charles, "Is this underground railroad?"

The woman stopped and spun at Werner. Charles craned his neck to glare at him around Ray's slumped head. Werner's face flushed under the scrutiny.

"Damn, Boom," Charles said. "This a bawdy house."

Werner gratefully watched the woman's blazing stare shift from him to Charles.

"Bawdy house? Charles, you all wrong." She turned and headed down the corridor lined with doors, faster now.

"What the hell, underground railroad," Charles scoffed.

Reaching the last door on the right, the woman swung it inward and gestured with an open hand. "I'll be downstairs, but if you find more trouble than you already got, don't come to me."

With that, she left the men standing outside the small room. It held a rumpled-sheeted bed, a dented brass spittoon, and an empty water basin. A thin layer of sawdust blanketed the floor. Werner and Charles squeezed through the door, dragging the slave hunter. They looked at the bed and dropped Ray on the wooden floor. Werner rolled his aching shoulders while Charles closed and locked the door.

Werner whistled. "Your friend Maggie."

"Maggie?"

"Maggie Spurlock, your friend. Though for five dollars, I was hoping at least for two beds."

For the first time since Werner had met him, Charles laughed. "She ain't Maggie Spurlock. Maggie Spurlock a key, Boom, just a word that gets the door open. But now you go on calling her Maggie. I don't think she'd want you knowing her name anyhow." Charles laughed again and then looked down at Ray, unmoving on the floor. Charles kicked the slave hunter in the small of his back. "He ain't waking up any time soon, and it ain't 'cause I hit him too hard. So drunk, he couldn't see a hole in a ladder."

Charles sat on the creaking bed, with Ray at his feet. The swift beat and a banjo's staccato twangs leaking through the floor from the dance hall below. Werner fetched the spittoon from the corner, and sitting down, offered Charles a cheek of his tobacco. They sat chewing in silence for some moments before Charles turned from the spittoon and spat across Ray's chest.

"If I learnt one thing stewarding and cleaning up on them boats, it's this. It ain't the spittin' that's a problem, it's the missin', you know, Boom?" Charles smiled a wide, tobacco-stained smile.

After that they both ignored the spittoon.

"Charles, this man, you keep saying he was there in January. The Garners?"

The two men, pushed close by the cradling, creaking bed, looked at each other. Charles spat again across Ray's chest. "Too right. That bitch-born twig was there."

"What happened?"

"You don't know about them Garners?"

Werner shook his head.

"You got to read a newspaper doesn't have your name

in it some time." Charles sighed and wiped a hand down his face. "The Garners. There was six of 'em, Robert and Margaret and their four kids." Charles winced at the memory. "Mary, Thomas, Samuel, and the baby, Priscilla. Little 'uns. None of 'em more than five or six. They escape a plantation over Boone County with a group and come over here when the river was froze up. Remember last winter, it was so cold? Walked over, like it was cobblestone, and went to her cousin's house near here. The owner, name 'a Archibald Gaines, he notices they gone pretty damn quick, account 'a he's been fucking Margaret regular for years. So, he's on his horse with the marshal and this sack of shit," Charles buried a toe in Ray's side, "and some of those other soul-stealers. They come right over here. And they know where to look. Mean and ignorant, but not as dumb as we'd like 'em. They start pounding on the cousin's door, telling 'em all to come out and go back to being slaves, like what any sensible nigger should do, but Margaret, she decides different. Takes her a kitchen knife, and. Well. She got Mary 'cross the neck. She died fast. Two years old. The other ones she stuck, but not killing-deep.

"*Mein Gott.*"

Charles snapped wet eyes at Werner. "Maybe it's better you don't read the paper, Boom. Nicer for you not to know. She had a choice, and she made it." Charles leaned back on his elbows, stared at the ceiling, spoke to himself. "First time I saw Cincinnati, I was still property. Of Theophilus H. Rhodes. I was a goddamn overseer, too. Thought I could prove to this man that I'm also a man. Damn pride is what it was. I was bringing a group to his brother's plot over here in Kentucky, since he's got some debt on him back in Virginia and he don't want it collected in the form of us. You know, for our sake, so we don't get sold south, he says. We stop in Cincinnati along the way, no one looking over us but me, no chains, nothing. Some folk came on the boat and say, 'You get off here, you's free. No slaves in Ohio. And close to Canada, too.' Nah. Nuh-uh. Not for overseer Charles. I corralled them and convinced 'em, said you work hard, you lend a hand, and soon, you'll see. Besides, what's up in Canada? Snow? Not a single man or woman, outta group of thirty, took those steps down the gangplank, not a one. On my word, because of me."

"You are here now, free. At least this Rhodes he sets you free."

A hoarse laugh set off from Charles' belly and clawed out from his throat. "Rhodes never set no one free his whole life. Don't believe in it."

Werner and Charles both stared straight ahead at the stained wall bulbous with peeling paper.

"Even free, up here, the only doors open to me in Ohio are at the jail and the penitentiary. It wears you down. All of it. Like them little islands we get in the middle the river. The current grabs at you. You get ate up, a bit every day, 'til they take you off the map. The pilots forget you was ever there. Then you take a runaway and get him to freedom, see his back straighten as he's marching north in the darkness. It's like a dam burst upstream, and the debris all comes down and builds you up again. You get bigger, ready to drown them same pilots forgot you was there."

"Captain Walker, he understood this?"

Charles nodded, looking at his feet. "Dell understood. When we was down there Louisiana, he'd be tellin' people I was his slave."

Werner raised his eyebrows.

"Nah, it's good," Charles said. "Meant I could get off the boat for a spell, see a bit of town without being terrified the whole time. I'm his property, that means any man takes me, or kills me, he's committing a crime, crime 'a thievery. And they punish that down there, sure as shit. If I'm just a free black man, taking me, killing me, that's regular business." Charles spat a line of tobacco juice across Ray's chest.

Werner made it an X.

"When Cap'n Dell first took over the boat from big Dell we was on a run from New Orleans, same as we do every month. But someplace Arkansas way this little dinghy comes out to the middle of the river, where it's deep. Current there good enough take that whole dinghy right down to the Gulf. They light up a lantern and start waving, frantic. Right there, nine outta ten, shit, ninety-nine outta hundred keep right along. Could be bandits. Best case, they looking for something from you, which is just what most captains don't wanna give. Dell, he heaves to, and before he can say nothing, there's three jimmies on our deck, all wide-eyed and shivering in their torn-up clothes. A couple 'a white folk in the dinghy, they toss up a bag of silver, fifteen dollars Dell told me later, and say take these boys to Newport—that's Indiana, you understand. Keep your fee, they say, and leave them the rest."

Ray groaned and rolled to his side. "Bullshit," the slave hunter managed between dry heaves. "Where you brung me?"

Charles stood and kicked Ray fiercely in the belly.

"It is a bawdy *Haus*," Werner said, smiling.

Standing over Ray, Charles hissed, "Why'd you kill Cap'n Dell?"

Between shallow gasps, Ray attempted a reply. "Fuck—

is—Captain—Dell?"

When Charles moved to kick him again, Werner stood and stepped between them, holding a hand to Charles' chest. "Charles, you get tobacco on your shoe. And you. Captain Delphebus Walker, the captain of *High Water*. Dead two days after you visit him."

Ray pushed his chest off the floor and shoved his back against the wall, propping himself with his legs splayed in front of him. He looked down at the tobacco stains veining his shirt, furry with the floor's sawdust. "Oh, now, what the hell—"

"I am not deputy," said Werner. "Charles is not marshal. There is no judge. You convince me you did not kill Captain Walker, or we kill you and get a drink."

"Whoa, now. Whoa," Ray protested loudly, lifting his open palms. "Just, whoa. I ain't kilt no one. Not in a little bit here."

"He's lying," Charles said.

Ray stiffened and looked up at Charles. "Boy, you call me a liar again, I'll tie you to my horse and see how fast you can run."

Charles raised a fist, and Ray's hands flew up around his face. Charles sat down with half a smile. "Shoulda shot this man outside. We'd be done by now."

Ray ran his hands through his hair and lowered them slowly. "Now, you," he focused on Werner, "you knew my name, but look," glancing back to Charles, "back home, I'm the law."

Charles snorted. "This a waste of time, Boom."

"What I mean is, I'm just a constable. Arrestin' all the slaves and niggers, that's part of my business, a big part. Judge sees 'em, and I get paid. Sixty-two and a half cents, each one I catch. And same again each one I flog, used to be. Now it's fifty cents, whole show. So, some man got himself a whole plantation wants to pay me handsome come up here and fetch his run-off jimmy ... shit, that's how the world spins 'round." He shrugged. "But murder a white man? This *is* a white man y'all are talking about?"

Werner sighed. "*Ja.*"

"No sense in that. No sense." Ray shook his head. "That's sin."

Charles was shaking his head, glaring at Ray.

"And if that white man helped slaves to be free?" Werner asked Ray.

"Free? Better for them they just stay put, but shit, if they ain't gettin' free, how am I gonna get paid to fetch 'em back?"

Charles pushed himself from the bed and balled his fists, but he was stayed by the sound of many pairs of boots ascending the stairs from the bar. All three men turned their heads toward the noise. Werner could hear an angry crowd through the thin walls careening down the hall.

"What room is it, Dani?" someone said.

"Damnit, Shad, stop! I'll buy you a drink downstairs—all of you. Drinks on me!"

"What room, Dani."

A brief silence, then the sound of wood splintering and a door exploding open, followed by a high scream and a low, muffled yell.

Ray had pushed himself into the corner behind the door and was frantically searching his pockets. "Where's my gun?" He glared up at Werner. "You got my gun?"

Werner shook his head, his attention still out in the hall. Another crash, another scream. They were moving down the hall closer and closer.

Ray looked around the room. He lowered his head to see under the bed. "My rifle. Where's the rifle?"

"At the bar," Werner said and then put a finger to his lips. He pulled his revolver and slowly cocked the hammer. Charles drew out the small, two-barreled pistol from his pocket. They leaned against the door on either side of the frame, listening to the voices yards away down the hall.

"Next one, now, Dani. 'Less you wanna tell me where they at. No?"

"Shadrach! Damnit!"

Werner looked down at Ray, cowering in the corner, trying to push himself through the wall, back to Virginia. "Convince me you did not kill Dell Walker."

"Jesus Christ, who?"

From outside, "There's only so many rooms, Dani," the man said. "I'll jus' kick 'em all down."

"All right, shit," said Ray in a tight whisper. "When did he die?"

"Last week," Werner replied.

"Last week, when?"

"Found on Wednesday, killed Tuesday."

Ray sucked through his teeth. "Goddamn, Tuesday? Tuesday I was 'round. Damn, I don't know. I'm drunk! It wasn't me!"

"Bullshit," said Charles.

From the hallway, a new voice, "Shad, down the end!"

The trampling came their way, fast. Werner, gripping the pistol, looked at Ray, whose beseeching eyes searched out some escape.

"I believe him," Werner said.

Charles spun from the door and stared at Werner.

"Believe him?"

Before Werner could respond, the door burst from its hinges.

8
The Water

Chin pinned to his chest, Werner squinted his eyes against the sun and studied the stain on his pantleg. It was a speckled constellation stretching between hip and knee. When he picked at the largest blotch, his fingernail came away a bright red.

He rolled his eyes away from his hand stained with Ray's blood, and looked around. He strained to remember arriving there. The dry craters of an alley's brick wall came in and out of focus. Pawing the rough, mortared grooves, Werner pulled himself to a seated position. The wall lurched, and the ground lifted. He turned his head and emptied his stomach. The retching exhausted him, and he fell to his back, where the world stopped sloping and bucking. He pried one eye open and quickly closed it against the garish blue sky. Fragments of the night before came back to him, making him scowl.

The door to their room at the brothel booted inward,

pushing Werner onto the bed. Charles stepping back to reveal in the hallway a group of men, hot with the flushed excitement of drink, knives and batons bobbing in the wake of bodies. The man who had kicked in the door standing impassively on its remnants holding a shotgun aimed at Ray.

Someone shouting, "I told you it were him," the echoes from around the room and down the hall, many voices clamoring to be heard at once. Something wet splattering against Werner's face after a blast filled the room. His ears pounding, ringing. His eyes stinging from smoke.

Clearly now, behind closed eyelids, Werner saw what remained of Ray heaped in the corner, sagged and turned out. The slave hunter's mouth and eyes gaped. The man with the shotgun turned and shouldered his way through the throng and down the hallway.

Werner remembered Charles pushing him through the small crowd, each onlooker elbowing for a view of the dead slave hunter. They retraced their steps to the door downstairs, passing along the way the gunman, now holding a bottle of whiskey at the bottom of the landing, ogling the bottle glassy-eyed as the two men passed.

"Get out of here," said Charles.

The man said nothing.

"Ain't nobody coming here for him," said Maggie, or not-Maggie. Werner remembered someone calling her Dani. "Shad, you're gonna help get that pile of nothing dropped on the levee. Then you can spend the night here. Pickett gonna want to talk to you." She rested a hand on his shoulder as she passed him going down the stairs. "And you two." She advanced on Werner and Charles. "Where's my money?"

Outside, they turned different directions, Werner north and Charles south. Werner stopped and looked up at the brothel's walls. "You are happy with this?"

Charles sighed and turned around. "I ain't sad about it."

Werner nodded. He was about to start on his way when he asked, "What happened with those slaves Captain Walker picks up in Arkansas?"

"Dropped 'em north of the river."

Werner remembered seeing Charles' teeth, bright in the night's gloom.

"All of 'em together started laughing and singing, shit, middle of nowhere. And Dell says, from now on, we do that as often as we can."

Werner kept nodding, then turned and trudged north, looking for a bar.

In the searing light of the next morning, across the street from the alley where Werner woke up, the lacquered wooden doors of St. Mary's proclaimed against the church's whitewashed walls. The sun blazed directly at him, but at least it would be cool in there, the light filtered by stained glass.

"Brothers, sisters, it is a fine thing to see so many of you joining us this morning—a stout and hale body is only possible with a healthy soul."

Werner attended often enough to recognize the Czech-accented German of Father Clement Hammer. Even slumped in the penultimate row, Werner felt assaulted by his sonorous voice.

"Today we sang hymns, we joined together in the presence of our Lord, and we fulfilled a holy sacrament by partaking of the body of the Christ."

Werner groaned. Too late for altar wine.

"And we prayed. We reached to almighty God with our thoughts and our feeble voices, imploring Him to hear us and to heed us. But answer me this and be not afraid of honesty's sting—for whom did you pray, brothers and sisters? Was it for your neighbor? For your fellow man? The needy, the disadvantaged? Or was it for your own desires—what you deem, in the inevitable shallowness of our mortal lives, your needs?"

Werner watched the collection of heads in front of him nod along with Hammer's sermon. The motion brought back his nausea. Last night's lagers wringing him dry. He squeezed his eyes shut hard and swallowed back the bile. He awoke with a start when the reverend pounded the lectern with a fist, his voice rising above the murmurs of the congregation.

"We must endeavor for more," the reverend intoned. "We must. We are Europeans in a new and foreign land, God's children in a world of temptation and vice. We fled persecution, hardship, and intolerance, only to find what? Persecution, hardship, and intolerance. And *opportunity*. Take the opportunity, brothers and sisters. Take it with all the force and energy you possess. Leave the rest." He swept his gaze across his audience. "When I first came here from Jáchymov sixteen years ago, I traveled with my brother, Johann. We needed little, but had less. We struggled—like many of you here today. We begged, took work where we could find it, and like so many before and after us, we resorted to thievery and to vice."

Werner closed his eyes, to better concentrate on Hammer's words, but as his jaw slackened and his head slid back, he soon caught only pieces.

"... summer morning ... Covington ..."

His head snapped up.

"... wandering the fine cobbled streets. Like today, the sun insistent, taking its tithe of sweat and making a dry waste of our tongues."

Werner felt his own swollen tongue, as if made for a larger mouth, sticking to his gums.

"My brother grew quiet, and I followed his eyes to a home across the street. A beautiful home ... bowl of water ... his face and chest ... last drop fell to his tongue."

Werner's forehead cracked into the pew in front of him. He lurched back in his seat, the pain in his head now keeping him awake.

Hammer held a long silence, looking out over the congregation, then continued, quieter. "It was not until we were back on the ferry that his stomach began cramping. Halfway across the river, he could not move from the railing, where he retched again and again and again into the uncaring water. The other passengers looked up or down or across the river, but none stared for long at a young, foreign man gagging and crying, writhing through the last moments of his life." The reverend's natural frown deepened as he raised a hand to the heavens. "With God's divine guidance, I was able to find the truth of my brother's death." He lowered his hand to his mouth and shook his head. "Amelia Trully lives with her husband and two grown children on South Street in Covington. She tends to a wondrous garden behind her iron fence. Mrs. Trully's lilies had been eaten on a handful of occasions by a neighbor's dog, whose owners proved unwilling or unable to curb the cur's appetite. Mrs. Trully saw only one way to decisively deal with this situation

—with a bowl, a few cups of water, and an ample portion of arsenic."

A shudder went through the congregation.

"Each of you here is hot. Each of you here is dried out and parched. But I say this to you: Do not drink the water, for it is poisoned! Do not trade everlasting peace for desires masquerading as needs. Hold on dearly to your true selves, heed the word of God, and *take* the opportunity. May the almighty God bless you. The Father, and the Son, and the Holy Spirit."

Mumbled voices joined together to form an audible "Amen," and Werner was finally enveloped in silence. His sweaty palms cradled his sweaty face, and he focused his attention on not being sick again. He felt the pew next to him sag.

"The Hammer. That story gets worse every time he tells it."

Werner recognized her voice and spoke without lifting his head.

"Good morning, Fraulein Linck."

"Werner," she said, a reprimand.

"Good morning, Bettina." Werner had yet to remove his face from his hands.

"The last time I heard it, the dead man was his cousin," Bettina said. "The first time I heard it, he was just some man."

Werner spoke into his own lap. "It is no good wrong-mouthing a priest in his own church."

"Then we will wrong-mouth him elsewhere. There are benefits to owning a brewery."

"Your father owns the brewery."

"My father owns the brewery." She paused, deepened

her voice, and said in English, “A man’s worth is his work, Bosenbach, and if you won’t work, you’re not worth shit.”

Werner lifted his head. “A man doesn’t make a profit; profit makes him a man.”

“The dollar is God’s finest creation.”

“If it bleeds money, shoot it.”

“It’s guts and gumption you need for work—leave the heart at home with your wife.”

Werner rocked back as they shared a hearty laugh, drawing reproachful stares from scattered parishioners still praying. “Gumption. That is good. You are becoming a real American, Bettina,” Werner whispered. The laughter had brought nausea with it. He took as deep a breath as he could.

“That is what we are here for.” Slipping back to English, she said, “OK, stubborn Dutch bastard, come, have a beer.”

They walked north, Bettina stopping every few feet to greet passersby or rap on a glass front window and wave at the proprietors inside. They were mostly artisans—wood turners, chairmakers, fitters, chandlers, and cobblers. On other days, this dance would wear on Werner’s nerves, but the glad-handing gave him opportunities to catch his breath, and to pull the sticking shirt from his back. At the corner of Liberty and Clay, Bettina stepped into a bakery and emerged with warm, sliced *schnecken*, handing one to Werner.

“Not as good as lager, but it will keep you standing until we get there.”

Werner bit into the warm dough, finding the familiar syrupy cinnamon and walnut mixture turn to something acrid and endlessly dense in his mouth. He vomited as they crossed Liberty, Bettina apologizing to a carriage whose progress was halted by Werner's convulsing form. She made no mention of the incident as they turned onto Hamilton Road, its cleaving diagonal cut a welcome to the Northern Liberties, the eleventh and twelfth wards, a messy appendage splaying to the steep wall of hills north of the city's gridded streets.

The F. Linck Brewery stood taller than its neighboring buildings by one layer of decorative masonry. The wide, double wooden doors were open, and Bettina led Werner past rows of many-limbed metal contraptions whose mute exteriors hid bubbling, furious innards of hops and yeast. Down a ladder through a crude hole in the factory's floor, Werner found the first relief of his day. The *felsen,* a long tunnel strung with small lanterns and filled to the ceiling with wooden barrels of lager, was at least thirty degrees cooler than the June day outside. He inhaled deeply and let his hand glide along the barrels' exteriors as they moved deeper into the tunnel.

"My favorite place in the summer," Bettina said.

"*Ja,* you belong here, I think," said Werner.

Bettina tilted her head, inviting the rest.

"These barrels were also made by your father, and they, too, are full of shit."

She laughed. "You can insult me, Bosenbach, but not the lager. It is the finest in the West."

"I am easy to convince."

Bettina filled two steins from a tapped barrel. Werner took one and gripped it firmly, hoping to cover the tremors running through his hands.

"*Zum Wohl.*" Werner drank his mug down in urgent gulps and wiped his face with his sleeve. "You were right. Best I've ever had."

Bettina balanced her still-filled stein on the curving belly of a barrel. "Why do you not take my father's offer?"

Werner said nothing.

"We all owe—"

"You owe me nothing." Werner reached for Bettina's stein but was halted by a shot to his shin from her pointed boot. He winced, and she took his stein to the tapped barrel.

"You protected us."

"That's just a story, Bettina."

She turned and handed him his refilled stein.

He immediately raised it to his lips.

"You should have a job."

Exhaling after a long pull, Werner said, "I do have a job."

"Collecting Lafcadio Murphy's money. Didn't you come here for a new start?"

"I came here so I would not have to mine mercury. There is no mercury here—I do not go down into the *Dreikönigszug* to be buried. I am a true story of American success."

"You could use your story to convince saloons to sell our lager."

"My story." Werner finished his beer, feeling revival around the corner. "Who needs it to sell the best lager in the West?" Before she could respond, he said, "You know, I was in a negro brothel last night."

"What?"

"It's true. If you ever want to go, try the name Maggie Spurlock, but maybe don't mention me." A smile spread across Werner's face as he watched Bettina decide if he was joking. It was extinguished by the thought of Bixby Ray. He had to speak with Sophia Walker. "I have to go to Covington."

"Kentucky?" She shook her head. "Father is hosting a party at Grammer's tonight. Come. You can talk about what you could do here."

Werner turned back to the tunnel's exit and the day's heat.

Her voice chased him down the *felsen*. "There will be beer."

9
The Money

On the Covington ferry, out from under the brick and wooden towers that grew in Cincinnati like fungus on a rotting log, he could finally see the sky. Not bisected by a clothesline, stabbed by a church steeple, or hidden behind a roof, but stretched out above him. The indifferent, swirling clouds hurried east, directly against the tide of humanity.

At the ferry's bow, Werner filled his lungs with cool river air, and felt the river's insistence west. The boat slid under his feet. The rear wheel slapped muddy and roiled water. The Ohio surged down an invisible hill, battling soggy banks in jogs and lengths to find a distant delta on which to disgorge and settle.

He told himself: Take the money.

He stared down at the water, split into a rippling arrowhead against the wooden prow below him. This river carried fortunes on its apathetic back, depositing riches at this fortuitous bend like so much silt. It was an icy path to freedom or a cold, gasping plunge into a casket. It was a finish line and a starting point, a goal, a disappointment, a south-flowing threat. To Werner it was water and mud and blood. The same as everywhere else. It made him nauseous. He scraped at the darkened red stain under his fingernail, and thought: Take the money.

Werner knew where the widow's house should be, but when he got there, he knew it wasn't right. The many-coated paint was green, not brown, and the pillars scalloped, not smooth. He turned and walked, turned and walked, turned and walked, looking over his shoulder at the wary pedestrians looking over their shoulders at him. He strode the wrong neatly macadamized streets and watched the wrong homes stretch to fill unthinkably large lots. He found the Walker house on a street he promised himself would be the last he searched before retreating Over the Rhine for a lager. Tasting the amber passing over his tongue, he felt his shoulders droop in disappointment at the sight of the widow's home. The sun crept close behind him and burned against Werner's neck. It prodded him forward, up the wooden stairs and past the columns, relenting finally in the shade of the front porch. Werner rapped the door with his knuckles and hoped to hear nothing. Instead, the sound of heavy footfalls advanced on him from inside.

The door opened, and there stood a man he did not know. Werner took half a step back to survey the house, worrying that these massive homes might stalk around at night like nocturnal predators, bedding down wherever dawn found them.

The man spoke through patchy facial hair. "Are you him?"

Werner opened his mouth, but the man spat at his feet.

"Yeah, you're him."

Sophia's voice emanated from within. "Minard, who's there?"

The man stared at Werner.

"Minard!"

"It's your Dutchman," Minard called over his shoulder. He turned back to Werner. "Thought you'd be bigger."

"Bring him in." Sophia's voice cracked with frustration.

Minard made no move. "You find who killed my brother?"

Over Minard's shoulder, Werner saw Sophia emerge in the hallway. Dressed still in black, she stood with her hands pressed against her hips. "Minard."

"I ain't your butler," Minard said. "And he can talk good enough out there."

Werner leaned to one side to seek out Sophia's eyes. "Frau Walker. I have news."

She sagged minutely before reasserting her posture. "What news? Minard!"

Minard flinched, then turned slightly, allowing Werner a small space through the door. Werner took it and more, landing a heavy shoulder against Minard as he passed.

Sophia invited Werner into a small library. She seated herself behind a dark-wood desk in a chair that engulfed her narrow frame. Werner, surrounded by rows of leather-bound volumes, wondered about all the world's knowledge he would never have. Minard followed them in and leaned against a shelf. Sophia passed over Werner an examining gaze that made him suddenly aware of his odor—whiskey, sweat, iron. His hand moved to cover the bloodstains on his pants.

"Tell me." She searched Werner with beacon eyes.

Werner remained standing, and turned away from the widow's scrutiny. "We found a man named Bixby Ray. A slave hunter. He is dead."

Sophia lifted her hands from her lap to the desk, then returned them to her lap. "A slave hunter."

"*Ja.* Bixby Ray. From Virginia."

Werner watched her face fall into slackness. He thought of the certainty and revulsion he had felt when a man with large, rough hands came to his door in Weichweiler to tell him his father was buried in the mine. Werner, ten years old and half the man's height, could not stop staring at the dirt caked on this man's hands, compressed under his nails. That dust, that nuisance, had killed his father?

Minard was shaking his head. "What would a slave hunter want with Dell?"

Werner, grown again, aching and itching and sweating, needed a moment. He thickened his accent to say, "I am sorry. Please could you repeat?"

Minard sneered. "Did they get in a fight?"

"You have heard of underground railroad?"

"Shit, I heard of it," Minard laughed. "Like I heard 'a Salmon Chase." His voice quickened. "What's it to Dell?"

Werner focused on Sophia. "This Ray made visit to your husband's boat. Two days before your husband was killed, this Ray was there. Your husband transported escaped slaves. Took them north. Charles believes—"

Minard cut him off. "Dell never *transported* no slaves."

Sophia's eyes were on her lap. "Minard."

"No, Dell ran a business. He drove the boats." Minard jabbed his finger at Werner. "What's he care about those niggers? What are you trying to do here?"

Sophia's voice grew sharper. "Minard."

"No," Minard said again. "What are you about? Trying to say Dell *transported* slaves. Part of the underground railroad—how stupid do you think he was? How stupid do you think we are?"

"I think there is difference between stupid and brave," Werner said. "Can be sometimes hard to see."

Sophia raised her head. "Which is it when you leave your wife alone?"

They stared at each other over the desk. Werner gripped his thigh, thinking: Take the money. Sophia shook her head and stowed a loose strand of hair behind her ear. She opened a drawer and withdrew a stack of wide bills.

Minard took a long, fast stride toward her. "Don't go givin' him any money, now."

Werner stopped Minard's advance with a hand to his chest.

Sophia watched them with a faint smile. "Minard, it's OK," she said. "I am finding new debts every day, like gray hairs. But this one I am happy to pay."

Minard slapped Werner's hand away and stepped closer to Sophia and the money. "You're not giving this pile of stacked Dutch shit a damned thing."

She lifted her eyes to his. "Why did you come, Minard?" Her voice was low.

Werner watched her hold the man in an unwavering stare.

"When we got married," she said, "you were not there. When we built this house, you were not here. When our child was born, you did not visit. When we christened a new boat, where were you? Cowering in St. Louis, sulking because you weren't one of the Delphebi, because your brother, who loved you, God help him, took what was his?"

"You don't know nothing about that," Minard said.

"He took it, and he made it better. Bigger. Like a son should. And he made it his, like a man should." She sagged. "And he helped people."

"Niggers?" The question came out of Minard's mouth with a high pitch of disbelief.

Sophia straightened like a rope pulled taut. "What did you bring with you, Minard? Did you bring any help for our debts?"

"They's your debts."

"You are damned right about that. What about know-how, did you bring that along? Four days from now, could you captain the *High Water* down to New Orleans and bring her back inside a month?"

"Well, I—"

"No, you couldn't. You didn't bring that with you because you never stuck around long enough to get it. Saw it was all Dell's to take, and you lit out. All you brought with you is your name and those grubby fingers out for what you think is yours." Sophia pushed her chair back, scraping along the floor, and stood. "I am a Walker, too. This will never be yours, Minard, because it is already mine." She pointed at the door. "Now get out."

Minard crossed his arms. "You don't tell me what."

"I do here."

Werner cast his eyes to Minard then back to Sophia, back to Minard, back to Sophia.

"Mr. Bosenbach," Sophia said, keeping her eyes on Minard. "I will give you twenty more dollars to batter this man about the face."

Werner shook out his hands. "I will do that for free."

As Werner advanced on him, Minard untangled his arms and took a few hurried steps back toward the door. "Damn it, Sophia," he said. Werner raised his fists, and the man fumbled to open the door, keeping his eyes on Werner. Finally, he slipped through and slammed the door behind him.

Werner turned to Sophia, seated again at the desk, counting the banknotes in front of her. "I swear to the merciful mother of Christ, if he woke that baby. ..." She shook her head. "The great goddamn Delphebi." She looked up at Werner. "You know they all named their first sons the exact same thing? Dell was the fourth. 'As long as there's been America, there's been a Delphebus Walker succeeding in it.' That is what his father used to say. Dell even started up with it. But there was no part of me on board with that. No son of mine was going to be a fifth, like some inbred royal." She stopped counting and lowered her head.

"Mrs. Walker," Werner began, feeling the spread of panic at his own decision. "This Ray, I am not certain—" He sighed. "He did not kill your husband."

Sophia's hands landed with a muted thud on the pile of bills in front of her. Her eyes narrowed. She gripped the desk. "Dell knew it was dangerous. I told him that. He knew and he did it and they got him." Something grabbed at her attention, and she smiled a little. "My daddy used to say, 'If you see a fox near the henhouse, don't go blaming the dog for dead chickens.'"

Werner, parched, swallowed and said, "What?"

Her faint smile was gone. "It means simple is good. Simple is usually right. Dell helped those underground railroad people—a slave hunter killed him. Why's that wrong?"

"Ray told me. I believed him."

"He told you. The slave hunter? That he didn't kill my husband. Who was smuggling slaves."

"*Ja.*"

"And then you killed him anyway?"

Werner's unfocused eyes saw Ray's blood billowing across the brothel's wooden floor, faster than he thought possible. "We were there when he died."

"So you didn't kill him."

Werner looked reflexively at the stain on his pants. "I didn't save him."

Sophia huffed a curdled laugh and glared at Werner. "Do not mistake me. You will not take from me more than what I owe."

Werner blinked.

"There's bigger and finer families in Covington, I know that. But you will not come into my home and use my—" Sophia exhaled abruptly. "My husband and this situation to your advantage."

"Mrs. Walker, I am ... what I am telling to you—"

"Is that you would like more money. Yes. I know. Amos warned me this might happen." Sophia sighed and looked at Werner a long while. She pushed forward the pile of bills. "Take this, Bosenbach, and leave."

"I do not understand."

"How long did you hope to string this out?"

"Frau Walker—"

"You will leave now."

Werner's grasp wrinkled the bills. Three hundred and fifty dollars. More than he had ever seen in one place before. He moved to the door, but stopped and turned. Sophia inhaled deeply through her nose and leaned away from him, defensive. He approached the desk and counted out a hundred dollars.

"I did not earn these," Werner said. "But I will."

Sophia turned away until he left the room. Werner heard her sobs begin as he stepped toward the front door.

10
The Councilman

If the killer across the street were trying to hide, he might have crouched behind the shading tree at the corner or the hedgerow further down. Instead he sat, as comfortable as a tall man gets on a knee-high wrought-iron fence, spitting at the brown tobacco stain growing on the pavement at his feet.

Werner's heels hit the wood of the widow's porch like a gavel. The man stood. There is a way a man looks when he can do violence and see no consequences. Werner had seen it before. He saw it now in this man's lean, stubbled face. The man started toward him. Werner felt the weight of the money in his pocket, and his face got splotchy warm. The man stiffened and reached into his coat.

Werner's hand dropped to his side. "That is tobacco you reach for in your pocket?"

The man turned, presenting to Werner his trim profile. "Same tobacco you got in that holster, Dutch."

"Hot today," Werner called.

The man looked up at the sun. "Gettin' worse."

By the time the man focused down from the sky, Werner had his pistol drawn. "I've shot men before, not knowing their name."

"Don't matter to me, Dutch. Spur that pony. See what happens."

"Let us say I continue down to the ferry. That way." Werner gestured with his chin behind him.

"I make you go another way."

"You have interest in where I go."

"Man pays me to have an interest in it."

Werner's heart clenched like a thrown fist, and now he wasn't sure if he'd checked the load in his gun recently. A tremor shortened his neck. If his first shot wouldn't go, he didn't trust this man to miss. He slid his pistol back to its holster.

"We're headed this way, Dutch." The man extended a thumb across his chest and waited for Werner to make the first move.

Werner looked north toward the ferry, saw himself back at Heinrich's paying off his slate, pushing a newly filled stein over to Otto. Instead, he stepped toward the man.

"Good choice," the man said, and gave Werner a soft push in the back, directing him east on Third Street toward Garrard.

The streets were clean and empty. Across a river from the largest concentration of Germans outside of Europe, and Werner couldn't find a single friendly face. They crossed Garrard, and the man let Werner go a few more paces before he coughed, directing Werner to their left. Surrounded by an intricate iron fence grounded in stone pillars, a two-story home coated in dazzling white paint perched atop a mound of closely manicured lawn.

"There's your door, Dutch."

Werner stepped up to a porch covered by a pressed-tin awning and pushed at the door. It swung inward, revealing a narrow hallway crowded by a steep staircase ascending against one wall.

A small voice came from his left, "Mr.— Herr Bosenbach?"

Werner spun, his hand slapping the handle of his gun. He saw a small boy with plastered hair in a tight-fitting woolen suit. The boy stood in a ten-foot doorway.

"My father would like to see you in the living room," the boy said, then turned and ran into the room behind him, out of view.

Werner followed him.

"You are a better listener than I expected, Bosenbach." Amos Shinkle sat on a couch, his arm extended around the boy. Shinkle smiled. It made him look uncomfortable. "A bourbon?"

He wanted to say yes. "*Nein.*"

The man who had ushered Werner to the house walked casually into the room, which prompted the boy to leap from the couch. "Gussington!"

The man kneeled and caught the onrushing boy by his shoulders. "Bradlingford! Are we strong today?"

The boy held up a flexed arm for inspection. The man squeezed the boy's bicep between thumb and forefinger and said, "Strong as ten men, Bradfordtons."

"Find your seat, Bradford." Shinkle stood and showed his back to Werner on his way to a cart between two tall windows that rippled with a distorted view of Cincinnati.

The boy ran back to the couch and flung himself into one of its corners.

Shinkle filled a tumbler and turned again to Werner. "Are you certain? I have ice. Fresh ice. No? Finest Michigan ice you can get. I have it carted right here to this house."

Werner looked to the man in the corner, whose hand was again jammed in his pocket.

"You want me to drink your whiskey, you don't need to have this man bring me here with gun."

Shinkle turned. "Who has a gun? Guss?"

The man in the corner took his hand from his pocket, gripping a tobacco pouch, and smirked at Werner. "I don't have no gun."

"I don't know Bavaria from, well, I can't think of another place over there," Shinkle said. "Prussia? But here, here in America, Bosenbach, when I ask people to come see me, it doesn't take a gun."

Werner drew his gun, cocked it, and pointed it at Guss. "I will have that whiskey. No ice."

The boy's mouth dropped open. He sat up bolt straight.

"Bradlingford, you go on now," Guss said.

"He'll stay right where he is," Shinkle said firmly. He moved closer to the boy and continued in a steady voice. "You stay right there, Bradford. But no talking, now." Shinkle straightened and took a long look. "That's wonderful, Bosenbach. You are just like Lafcadio said." Shinkle turned again to the bottles at the bar. "You have settled the matter of Delphebus Walker. I am glad. How did the widow take it?" Shinkle advanced on Werner, his fists filled with the bourbon glasses.

Keeping his eyes and gun on Guss, Werner accepted the proffered tumbler and poured the contents down his throat.

He held the empty etched glass out to Shinkle. "It is hard for her, being angry at a dead man."

Shinkle sat down next to his son on the couch, rattling his iced drink, a tinkling bell doomed by the heat to fade. Werner shrugged and let his glass fall from his hand, anticipating the shatter and the fine spreading rain of jagged edges. Instead, the glass landed with a firm thud and rolled in a rushed oval twice before it came to rest against the leg of Shinkle's couch.

"Good glasses," Shinkle said. "Solid. I get them sent in from London." He swirled his glass. "I find bourbon is proof final of God's existence and His presence in our lives. All we need, Bosenbach, all we can possibly want is right there in front us, if only we'd take it."

"Man's got gun on me," hissed Guss, "and you're giving him the bourbon-is-godly talk?"

As though Guss had never spoken, Shinkle lifted his glass at Werner. "To your good health."

Werner watched as Shinkle drank down the entire contents in two noisy gulps.

Shinkle exhaled satisfaction and pounded the tumbler on the low table in front of him. He waggled his eyebrows at Werner. "So, you kill a slave hunter in a darkie Cincinnati brothel, and a rich widow pays you for it."

Werner eyed Guss when he responded. "You know a little about a lot."

Shinkle smiled. It made his ears duck and sway. "You and I have both had good days." He stood and returned to the cart bristling with bottles and decanters, and spoke with his back to the room. "Put that iron away, Bosenbach. This is a celebration." He turned and lifted his newly filled glass. "To the completion of your *investigation*."

Werner made no move to holster his gun. "Is not complete," he said.

"You oughtn't be so sorry Walker's dead. Constituent of mine, yes, but, damned if the man wasn't stubborn. Thought what he did was special and different just because his daddy did it. Are you listening, Bradford?" Shinkle had returned to the couch. He grasped his son's knee. "This is important for you."

"Yessir," the boy said, staring at Werner's gun.

Shinkle followed the boy's eyes. "You know where I'd be if I just did what my daddy did? Up in the woods, north Brown County, skinning a squirrel for supper. That's only a few score miles up that way." Shinkle threw a hand in the air. "But compared to what you see here? I'd wager it's even further away than wherever you came from, Bosenbach." He took another clinking sip of bourbon. "I knew those Walkers. I came up from that river. I was eighteen, a cook on a flatboat, but a cook with vision. Doing the next thing before the right-now thing stops working. That's vision, Bosenbach, and it's a rare find in a man. Dell Walker didn't have it. Sentimental. Sure, the other steamboaters trusted him, let him do their negotiating. But he let himself get distracted by emotion and nostalgia. Me, the only time I don't bore myself is when I'm moving forward."

Werner grunted.

"Remember what we talked about? Quick work? Peace? You've done it, and iced the cake with a dead slave hunter. Of course your investigation is complete." Shinkle raised his eyebrows, waiting for Werner to agree with him. "I can help with some ways to spend your time, if that's what you're worried about. Fulltime work, keep you out of those packing houses this winter."

"You are the second person today to offer me job," Werner said. He started for the door.

Shinkle stood. "You gotta pick up a map and find your way to 'yes,' Bosenbach. On behalf of the city council of Covington, Kentucky, let me thank you for the service you rendered one of our citizens. I trust this will be the end of it."

Werner landed his pistol home in its holster. "Not the end." He was on the porch with the screen door clacking behind him when he heard Guss call out.

"Be seeing you, Dutch."

11
The Train

At Schierberg's on the Landing, Werner turned one of the widow's Kentucky bank bills into a jug of whiskey and pulled at it as he walked toward the *High Water*, still docked and awaiting its first run to New Orleans. The boat's newness stood out in the early evening light: white paint uncracked, ungrayed, its name blazoned in unfaded blue shadowed by a bold red border arching across the paddlewheel housing. He swallowed more whiskey, confronted by the boat's size, its air of authority and success. Werner knew, though, the bigger the steamboat, the more people would die when it blew up. It happened every year. The deaths were laid at the feet of firemen deemed overeager in their feeding of the boiler flames, or blamed on rambunctious young captains taking as much care of their charge as a child with a toy in a tepid tub.

Jesse, the ship's mud clerk, emerged from the covered main deck and stepped onto the bow.

"Ahoy," said Werner, lifting his jug.

The boy looked around him and then raised a middle finger at Werner before stalking back to the enclosed storage area. Werner grinned and took another pull of whiskey.

"You have a way of making friends, Boom," Charles called from the railing of the boiler deck.

Werner held up a flat hand to shade his eyes.

Charles waved him up. "I'll get you a glass to go with that."

Werner ascended to the boiler-deck parlor.

Charles perched on one of the elevated shoeshine chairs. He clinked two low glasses together in invitation. "Here to remember the good times?"

Werner heaved himself into the chair next to Charles, balancing his feet on the two brass pillars. He uncorked the jug and filled the glasses. "What good times?"

"Hell of a pour, Boom." Charles lifted his glass in Werner's direction.

Werner already had his to his lips.

"Celebrating?"

Werner looked at his now-empty glass. "Sophia Walker paid me."

"We done what she hired you to do."

"I did not earn this money."

"You could fill this river with the money 'round here hasn't been earned. What I think? You haven't been paid enough."

"She gave me three hundred and fifty dollars," Werner said.

Charles coughed. "I take it back. You been paid enough."

Werner tried a laugh, but it came out twisted into a sob.

He looked around the room. Empty of passengers, the room's luxury and pomp seemed like a trap. "What does Bliss say?"

Charles scoffed. "Gave me a pat on the back and a long list of things need doing before we set off on Sunday. He's off at a meeting with city council. Something Dell set up, but ..."

"*Ja.*"

"Only thing that makes sense, Boom, Ray killing Cap'n Dell."

Werner refilled his own glass.

Charles held his out. "Only a couple fingers, Boom. Not the whole fist."

Werner poured, and seated next to each other like regents granting an audience to the empty tables, they shared a silence.

"Some things just need doing," Charles said.

Werner nodded. "Some things." He slurped at his whiskey and closed his eyes to the horizon moving in the parlor's window.

"You want to hear something, Boom? Something funny?"

"*Ja.*"

"Some time ago, I was helping this fella north. Had to get him from the levee here over to Ripley, where he could get a cart that would take him ... that don't matter much. He'd just gotten free. Slave his whole life, about nineteen now. Lighted out on his own, and as we're making our way over to Ripley, he tells me this story."

Charles knocked Werner's arm with his empty glass. Werner filled it and his own.

"He's alone and traveling by night, and by the sixth

night or so, he's getting tired, so he figures he's dreaming on his feet when he sees these two eyes looking at him. Two burning eyes in the night. He just looks back, stuck there. And those two eyes, they start getting bigger and bigger, closer and closer, and they're making a terrible noise. Right at the last second, he jumps back, and the eyes swing past him carrying behind 'em a bunch of lit-up windows." Charles laughed. "It was a train. He'd never seen one before, and it nearly killed him. But you know what he says to me? Standing there watching the train go by, all he could think was, this some kind of demon creature taking souls to hell." Charles sipped his whiskey and smiled. "Damn, I go to hell, I hope it's by train! Ain't a slower way to get there. Anyway, so he's standing there, hid behind a tree watching these souls be carried off to hell, and he starts smiling and feeling pretty good. He's feeling all bucked up." He flashed at Werner a wry smile. "You know why?"

"*Nein.*"

"'Cause he notices, all them souls, the ones headed to hell in that creature's belly? They all white!"

Werner's weak exhalation joined Charles' bark of laughter. "Ray did not kill Captain Walker," Werner said, the words eliding and slurred.

Charles slapped his open palms on brass armrests and stepped down from the raised chair. "The man is gone. Gone is where he should be. You take that money and drink it straight down, all I care. But don't come in here to find sympathy for a slave hunter."

"Charles—"

"I'm sorry for your troubles, but we done what we set out to do. It's over. Time to get back to business. Me to mine. You to yours."

"*Ja.* OK." Werner stood, suddenly exhausted. His legs tangled in the shine stand's footrest, and his face mashed against the salon's thick carpet.

Charles looked down at Werner as he managed to turn himself onto his back like a bug about to be crushed. Werner extended a hand upward. Charles reached down, but avoided Werner's hand, and picked up the jug of whiskey instead. Then he turned and walked out of the room.

Werner pulled himself up using the shoeshine stand as scaffolding. Through the cabin's porthole, he saw the evening's reddened sky marbled with cloud. He wended through the narrow maze between gleaming, cushioned chairs and linened tables, suddenly desperate to be outside, feeling buried in that dark room, buried like a mine. He struggled with the door, pushing and pulling, jerking, finally spilling out onto the hurricane deck, the shadowed and empty porch that wrapped around the boat's front.

He found Charles in a creaking rocking chair, smoking a pipe.

"Do you have my whiskey?"

Charles squinted at Werner through the screen of smoke he released through pursed lips. "Sure." With his foot, Charles pushed the jug of whiskey. It wavered on a bottom edge, fell, and rolled.

Werner lunged to his knees and grabbed it. He removed the cork and brought it to his mouth. Empty.

"River needed it more'n you, Boom."

Werner groaned and slumped into a chair next to Charles.

"Lookit there." Charles gestured with his pipe across the river at the dark mass of Kentucky.

Cradling the empty jug, Werner could detect a distinct

thickening of Charles' voice.

"That's how close it is. People out there. *Criminals.* Crawling under leaves and logs during the day, stumbling along at night. Criminals. Devils. Mad people. 'Cause they trying to steal *themselves.* Me, I'm sitting over here with a pipe and a jug, like I made it."

"If Ray did not do it, the killer could be after you, also," Werner said.

"You mean life could be dangerous for me in Cincinnati?" Charles laughed. Quieter, he said, "Any white man 'round here could just snuff me out and go home. That's this town. Dressed up like the North, ignorant and angry like the South, full 'a guns like the West."

Werner frowned. He felt a flush come to his face. The pair rocked in their chairs, listening to the screech of insects.

"But what's up in Canada, Boom, snow?" Charles loosed a hollow laugh.

Werner was thirsty. He eyed the growing darkness around him. "I have a party to go to."

12
The Bridgemaker

Pressing through the throngs in Grammer's *garten*, Werner could hear people whispering his name, the *ess* of Bosenbach scratching at his ears. His head felt gauzy. It was overfilled like a westward wagon, slow and creaking. In need of oiling. He headed for the bar.

A hand closed around his hip. He jerked away violently, squaring to confront his attacker. Bettina stood behind him, slack-jawed, a flash of hurt passing over her face before she could compose herself.

"Werner."

His name from her mouth settled his bursting chest. He felt a smile pulling at his face. "Bettina."

"This is Mr. Roebling," she said, in English, turning to allow a man Werner had not previously noticed to extend his hand. "He has been telling me about the most fascinating things."

The severe man leaned toward Werner and said, "You

are a world-historical man, Bosenbach."

Werner began his reply in German, having heard the man's accent, but Roebling held up his hand and stepped forward, obscuring Bettina from Werner's view.

"Let us speak in English. Every people demands of a foreigner, who wants to settle permanently among it—as I do, as I assume you do—that he will assimilate to his environment as soon as possible. The English language is the keystone in that foundation of assimilation, do you not think?"

Werner looked over the man's shoulder to Bettina. She smothered a grin and slipped away into the crowd.

"*Ja.*"

The man seemed unsure if he should take offense.

"Tell me, Herr—" Werner said.

"Roebling."

"*Ja*, Herr Roebling. Are *you* a wild historic man?"

Roebling squinted at Werner, hunting his face for the insult. "World. Historical. I studied with Professor Hegel in Berlin, and I apply his teachings to my life, my work. You know, in a state of freedom, ambitious men can pursue their passions and fulfill their promise."

Werner leaned toward the man. "The Professor Hegel? In Berlin?"

Roebling's lips widened the goatee hedgerow around his mouth into a smile. "You know his work. It is essential here. With the freedom we find on this land. ..."

Roebling's words cascaded from his mouth, building force. Bettina materialized holding three brightly painted ceramic steins. Werner gulped at his lager and let Roebling's speech fade to nothing. He thought about Dell Walker. Sophia wanted him to stop. Charles was certain it was done.

Werner had the money, folded snug into his jacket pocket. He looked at Bettina, nodding her head along with this Roebling's pretensions. He looked around the *garten*. He should find Linck the Elder and speak to him.

Werner was snapped out of his musings by something Roebling said. He interrupted, "Herr Roebling, could you repeat that?"

"It defies reason, yes," said Roebling, taking Werner's question as incredulity. "I submitted my plans for this bridge ten years ago this month. *Ten years*—in engineering this is a lifetime—and nothing. Ellet, he helped matters none. People hear about a suspension bridge, and they think about his disaster down in Wheeling. I wrote to him myself. Told him his bridge would need trusses and stays, or the first little gale to come along would destroy it. I take no pleasure in being proven right. I'll admit, in architecture he has some taste. But as a constructing engineer? He is a failure. I blame his French education."

"A bridge over the Ohio? Here?" Werner tried to imagine the span and saw only crumbling cobblestone splashing in thick, brown water.

"That is why I am here. Most of all I blame the politicians." Roebling gripped his chin. "Great are the men that have the will and accomplish something great. Politicians all want to accomplish something usual, something familiar. My bridge will not be familiar."

"I cannot imagine it," said Bettina.

"I can," Roebling replied curtly. "I have been imagining this bridge since I am seventeen years old. I look at the Bamburg bridge, you know it? Over the Regnitz, built with chain-links, the most beautiful thing I had ever seen. I sat down immediate and sketched it. The chains, they look like decoration, garlands, yes? Hanging between the guardians of the bridge, two towers of stone on either side. Immediate, to me, it is clear major errors were made in constructing this bridge. Now I fix those mistakes. Mine will be the world's longest suspension bridge." Roebling built with hands fluttering in the air the lines and angles of his bridge. "One thousand fifty-seven feet long, held aloft by more than ten thousand wire cables. Each cable, like this." Roebling curved his hand in front of his eye, making a C shape. "Ten-inch wire, a million pounds of it."

Struggling to fully return to the present moment, Werner gaped at Roebling. "Did you say something about steamboats?"

"*Ach*, ten years with my plan for the bridge and nothing. This beautiful bridge, in here," Roebling tapped his forehead. "And nothing to do. The steamboaters are just as bad as the politicians they own. They bought that surveyor cheap, and he declares my bridge will restrict the free navigation of the river Ohio. Scared my bridge will interfere with their business, so they come together and force their politicians to say no. But a civil engineer must be endowed with broad vision. He must look into the future and muster the force of character to override the shortsighted."

Werner was jarred forward by a hand on his back.

"Booming Werner Bosenbach!"

A man's grip on his shoulder turned Werner like a screw, and he came to see a face split wide by a smile. Georg Vennemann. Werner knew he would need more to drink.

"Bosenbach!" He extended his hand, but when Werner reached to shake it, Vennemann threw his arms around him instead and drew him into a tight hug. Before Werner could react, Vennemann was out of the hug and beaming at

Bettina and Roebling. "You're not meant to have favorites," Vennemann said in his fast, nasal German. "From the barber to the beer baron," he said, opening his eyes wide and lifting his eyebrows at Bettina, "all of one's constituents are important." Then he winked and slapped Werner's back. "But not every constituent gets you into office with a cannon!"

"I did not even cast a ballot for you, Georg."

"There's no avoiding it, Bosenbach. You got me in. That cannon of yours saved all those ballots with my name on them. Even if you did not cast one. Which," Vennemann opened his arms wide toward Werner, "I find hard to credit. Who else would you vote for?"

Bettina smiled, and Werner buried his face in his beer stein. "Councilman Vennemann, this is Johann Roebling," she said.

Vennemann pumped Roebling's hand, encasing it with two hands while searching his face. "Roebling, Roebling. Roebling! Not the bridgemaker, Roebling?"

"My business is in wire-making, Mr. Vennemann, but I do have a passion for bridge design. You might have heard of my Niagara—"

"What a day for you! Finally going ahead. Here to celebrate?" Vennemann didn't pause for a response. "Of course you are. Do you know the story of Booming Werner Bosenbach? Of course you do. Everyone knows. It was a year ago, a little more—"

"Georg." Werner had finished his beer. "Mr. Roebling has no interest in this."

"He also prefers English," added Bettina. "Keystone of assimilation."

Vennemann roped his arm around Roebling's back,

pulling him tight to his side. "No, that's not right. I get too much of that bird-chirping at the council. No, here at the *biergarten*, we speak like men." He released his grip of Roebling, who took a precautionary step away. "Excuse me, Bettina," he said bowing in her direction. "We speak like men and beautiful young women."

Bettina curtsied ornately. "Like men, beautiful young women, and sniveling politicians," she said with a smile.

Vennemann drew back and lifted his hand to his brow. In a high-pitched attempt at English, he bellowed, "I declare you to be *too* much, Ms. Linck, for this poor Southern belle."

Werner lifted his already-emptied stein to his face, while Roebling displayed a slack stoicism. Bettina did Vennemann the courtesy of chuckling.

Returning to German, Vennemann said, "That is my Southern belle. I believe it to be quite good."

Roebling coughed, leaned back on his heels, and looked around the patio as if he'd left his hat in one of the corners.

"As I was saying," Vennemann slid a convivial but tight-gripped arm around Roebling's elbow. "It was a year ago, a little more, and you could find the name *Georg Vennemann* printed on ballots all over this city. Along with a few other names, I suppose. Some men, they call themselves Know-Nothings." Vennemann scanned the eyes of his small audience with a growing smirk. "They knew enough to know they knew nothing, eh?"

Through the politician's wild guffaw, Werner could see the back of the man's throat.

"All the same," Vennemann continued, with his full attention back on Roebling. "These Know-Nothings, they think they have a patent on making Americans, and we don't fit the specifications. Get it in their heads that we're stuffing our ballot boxes." Again, he eyed Werner, Bettina, and Roebling in turn, letting them know a joke was on its way. "No more than usual, I can tell you." Vennemann brayed a satisfied laugh before tucking into the story again. "So, what do you do with a stuffed ballot box? If you're a Know-Nothing, you take it by force and light it aflame in streets. Happened in the thirteenth ward, and would have happened just the same here, if it weren't for that man, right there." Vennemann held out his arm, palm raised to the sky, inviting Roebling to take in Werner.

"I know how this one ends," Werner said. He stalked away through the crowd.

Behind him, Vennemann shouted, "You can still see the scars on his hands!"

Bodies packed in around Werner. He turned and bumped and shuffled his way to the bar. Why would people want to drink this way? Near impossible to find the bar, surrounded by words and bawdy laughter.

Bettina found him alone in a booth inside the deserted restaurant. "It's closed in here for the party," she said.

Werner wrapped his hands around the stein in front of him. "The bartender, he knew my name. Let me back here."

"Everyone knows your name," Bettina replied. "You should be out there. If people could just—"

"They know all they want to know."

She sat down in the booth across from him. "I don't."

13
The Riots

Werner had never told the story. By the time he woke up, after the newspapers had been pressed, the story was already told, indelible. He stood by as others recounted outlandish fiction, nodding and forcing a smile, adding a detail to everyone's delight, but never the whole thing.

"It was Election Day," he said.

Werner had cast a vote precisely once, in 1854, when promising to vote all the way down one side of the ballot had gotten him into a sweaty courtroom packed with raised hands and mumbled oaths. He'd come out American. A citizen, at least according to the judge.

"A citizen knows his vote is worth something when it's sought and bought," said the man who had brought him to court, slapping him on the back on his way out. "Congratulations."

American in theory. He was still Dutch in Cincinnati.

A year later, with nothing to gain from voting, he'd spent all of Election Day getting the kind of drunk you only know about the next day. Friedrich Yeager had told him to stop coming into the shop, the third job he'd lost in a year. He was late too often, drunk too often, and even when sober and on time, a clumsy and inexact carpenter. Werner had nodded along with these points, unable to disagree. They'd parted with a handshake, and Werner had more time to spend at the saloon.

Trading the quality of Over the Rhine's lager for Bucktown's lack of polling stations, Werner had started early at a saloon on Seventh Street. Down there, no one would ask him about Pap Taylor, or the Know-Nothings, or those pompous '48ers and their decision to consolidate the German vote.

Werner was finished drinking when he ran out of money, and when he left the saloon he was pleasantly surprised by the night's darkness. He crowded his mouth with a new plug of tobacco and decided with a sigh to turn toward his boardinghouse room in Over the Rhine, hoping the polls would be closed.

His path meandered north on Sycamore Street. A man stumbled toward him, one hand over his gut and another up to his face. Both hands seemed to be leaking blood. The man froze when he saw Werner only a few feet away.

Werner spat tobacco juice on the sidewalk. "Are you hurt?"

Hearing Werner's accent, the man started limping again. "You better get the fuck on," he said, his Irish lilt thickened by a fat lip.

The man passed by, Werner yelling at his back, "*Was ist los?*"

He answered without turning: "They're come to kill us again."

In the booth at Grammer's, Werner laughed. "The Irish," he said to Bettina, "they're here to make the rest of us look good."

She grinned only slightly. "Imagine what they say about the Dutch."

Starting north along Sycamore again, he was stopped by an echoing roar that made his shoulders jump and his feet scurry. When he was sure no one had seen his coward's waltz, he continued on, shaking his head at himself.

Turning onto Tenth Street, he saw the cannon first, a predatory statue, and then the men around it, shadows kicking at rubble around the *Enquirer* building. Crooking it in elbows and armpits, they jammed the sharp-edged lode into the cannon's mouth.

"Hurrah for Pap Taylor!" yelled one.

"The Dutch must be whipped!" said another, and they laughed.

"Damn the Dutch!" Werner yelled, causing the men to freeze and look up from the cannon.

"Who's there?" one yelled toward Werner. He leaned on a long ramrod. "American?" Mirth lingered at the sides of their mouths, ready to fade off.

"*Fick dich ins Knie!*" Werner yelled through his tobacco.

If the men around the cannon didn't understand Werner's insult, they heard enough to turn the cannon his way. Its small, dark mouth swallowed him whole. He saw a puff of smoke, heard laughter like crows cawing, and the air around him whistled before the cannon's report reached his ears. Craggy stones, moving too fast for Werner to see, bounced off the cobblestones at his feet.

Untouched and angry, Werner advanced. He closed the distance between as the men tried to reload. Werner felt clarified in his attack, sobered and calm.

"Away, you damned Dutch bastard!" yelled the one with the ramrod.

"Back to Dutch land, devil!" said another and forced a laugh.

Werner increased his pace, lengthening his strides. He could see the man plumbing the cannon's narrow depth with the rod, looking over his shoulder between jabs. The man dropped the rod and picked up a lit torch.

Fifty feet away, Werner stopped and spat. He jerked his chin at the men, and said, "*Scheisskerl.*"

"We warned you," the man yelled. The fuse hissed as he touched it with his torch.

A cavalry of stone galloped around Werner, engulfed now in sound and smoke. A flashing pain in his side quickly faded, and he continued his march.

Four men stood behind the cannon, struck mute and motionless by the sight of Werner emerging from the cannon's billowing smoke like he had caught the projected stones and held them in the fists at his sides.

The first gunshot came at Werner when he was twenty feet from the cannon. The man with the torch in one hand held out a revolver in the other. Like the first, the second shot missed, and with Werner ten feet away and still advancing, it set the three unarmed men off at a sprint. The man with the gun dropped the torch, added a second hand to the pistol's grip, and steadied it at Werner's chest.

As Werner stopped right in front of the man, the hammer plunged down, uselessly striking a faulty cap. Before the man could pull the hammer back again, Werner swatted the gun away and swung at the man's mouth with a balled hand that landed underneath his ear. The gun fell to the cobblestones, and the man bent and held his head with both hands.

Werner brought a knee to the man's face. They both fell to the ground. Werner seized the fallen revolver by its barrel, raised himself to his knees, and brought it down heavily on the back of the man's head. His hand stung from the impact, and the man crumpled with a breathy sigh.

It was quiet. Werner sprawled on his back next to the man, looking at the stars. They shifted and swung between buildings as he stared up. He remembered there being more, remembered his mother pointing at them all, telling him his father was up there among the bright lights, when Werner knew he was really buried somewhere under the same earth that had crushed and suffocated him.

He was surprised to raise his head and see the street deserted. He lurched up, stepping over the man. Werner slipped the revolver into his belt and picked up a bag that smelled warm and earthy. Powder. He retrieved the ramrod from where it had rolled, and lifted the still-lit torch. Looking from his filled hands toward the cannon and back, he dropped the ramrod and torch and began jamming his pockets with powder. Into the four pockets of his shabby jacket he packed the explosive. His thighs bulged gaudily when he stuffed his pant pockets, too.

He left the empty powder bag beside the man's gape-mouthed figure. He planted fuses into the button slits of his own waistcoat, then took up the torch. Werner went again on his way north, torch in one hand, the other dragging the cannon behind him on creaking wooden wheels.

Bettina interrupted Werner's retelling to ask, "That

man, he was dead?"

"The *Enquirer* says only, 'he came off second best.'" Werner shrugged.

She nodded and waited for Werner to continue.

The first few steps hauling the cannon were impossibly slow, but leaning forward with the rope digging into his shoulder, Werner found a steady pace. At the Walnut Street crossing into Over the Rhine, he saw illuminated by torchlight a swirling of men attached to batons and guns and fire. From cupped mouths came chants of "Damn the Dutch," "Remember Philadelphia," and "America for Americans!"

With their attention over the canal, Werner dragged the cannon to the rear of the crowd and collected a pile of loose paving stones and rocks. He fed the cannon handfuls of powder from his pockets, then crammed the shoddy ammunition into the beast's mouth, piecing together the weapon's workings from the firsthand tutorial he had received on Tenth Street.

He checked the revolver he'd taken and found three good cap-and-ball shots left. The handle, coated in sticky blood, clung to his palm. He tried to aim the cannon, but settled on a general direction, toward the mass of violence collected at his neighborhood's edge.

Werner lit the fuse. He saw some faces, hovering in torchlight, turn toward him before he retreated back down the darkened street. He braced himself for the explosion, crouching slightly. It did not come. The fuse was too long. Already, men were breaking from the large group and running for the cannon. Werner dropped the torch and cocked the revolver, resigned.

He watched as the men—all of them men, all of them white, all of them angry—neared the cannon, unaware of its lit fuse, which had burned down to the casing. One man circled to the cannon's rear. He had time only to wrench his head up in surprise before he, the cannon, and the group of men in front of it were enveloped in percussive smoke.

Werner was still holding out the revolver when the smoldering cannon scraped to a stop in front of him. He had put no blocks behind the cannon's wheels, and when it erupted, it flew backward as though ashamed of its part in Werner's ambush. The cannon dripped with fresh blood from tearing through the man who had been standing behind it. Smoke obscured Werner's view up the street, but he could hear the yells and cries of the rest of the mob. Desperate, Werner grasped the cannon by its scorching mouth. He heard the hiss of his flesh against the hot metal but felt nothing. He'd pushed the cannon ten agonizing paces when his hands came alive in searing pain. He managed to turn its metal bulk onto Court Street, the mouth facing the way he had come.

He reloaded the cannon, fishing fistfuls of powder from his pockets that left a stinging residue on his palms. Men started to stream past on Walnut, the flashing, clomping runners first, followed by the main section of the mob, indecipherable to Werner as individual men. All chasing the cannon's noise, none stopping to examine side streets. Werner bit a fuse, gnawing and pulling until it broke in two, slid it into the cannon, and realized he had left the torch burning on Walnut, surrounded now by feet and fists and weapons.

He held the muzzle of the gun to the fuse, closing one eye to solidify his target. One shot was enough to draw the mob's attention, but not to light the fuse. Werner recocked, trained, and squeezed the trigger. The revolver's bark and its puff of smoke were swallowed by the cannon's roar.

Within the flinty fog of cannon smoke, Werner awaited the rush. He had one shot left in the revolver, and he planned on using it. He thought he heard German, but could not be sure through his ringing ears. Then there was cheering, and he could see coming toward him men of Over the Rhine, recognizable in their bearded faces and rounded caps.

Men slapped Werner's back and shook his burned hands, but they were most interested in the cannon. Werner left them crowded around it, tucked the pistol in his pants, and started again on his walk home. Near the canal, a small man ran up to him and asked his name.

"That was the reporter," Werner said to Bettina. "He followed me from the start. It was the *Enquirer's* offices those men were cannoning when I found them."

"He got the right of it? That whole night?"

Werner shrugged. "I have these." He held up his hands to show the crescent moon scars across his palms. "From pushing the cannon's mouth. And this, too." He drew the revolver from its holster, placed the pistol on the table, and spun its handle toward Bettina.

She picked it up with two hands, turning and weighing it. She brought the grip close to her face and then looked to Werner. "Is that?"

"*Ja.* That is his blood. Hard to get off."

She held it up, pointed at Werner's mouth. He heard the gun's clap, saw the bullet punch his face and claw out the back of his skull, saw his emptying head land with a wet thud next to his beer.

"Werner?" Bettina had lowered the gun, fitting its barrel between the empty steins collected in front of Werner.

Her voice penetrated his fantasy.

"*Ja.*" He lifted a stein to his mouth.

"What you did was right."

"It was just something I did. I didn't think. I was angry."

"It was right." She placed her hand atop his. "Even if it did get Georg a seat on the council." She beamed at him, waiting for Werner to join in the joke, but his face remained slack, his eyes soft and pointed over her shoulder.

"Vennemann," Werner muttered before he shot up from his seat. He felt immediately a familiar shifting of his horizon. He rode it, hurling and careening the way he had come until he was again outside, bathed in damp sunlight, crashing through the blurred figures of the crowd, trying to find Georg. Werner spotted his permanent grin bobbing in the frothy sea of faces. He shouldered his way forward, losing sight of the councilman, then catching him again. He yelled out, "Georg!" and saw Vennemann's head swivel, scanning the party for an important face. Muttered oaths and the slap of beer spilling to the ground followed Werner as he bouldered through the crowded *garten*. "Georg!" he called again, inching closer.

Vennemann's eyes swung around and landed on Werner. His grin widened to a smile. "Werner—assure Mr. Roebling I've told him the truth." Vennemann still had a grip on the bridgemaker's arm.

Werner ignored Vennemann's plea, disregarded that pompous Roebling, and reached through the crowd to grip Vennemann's shirtfront and reel the politician in close, pulling and steadying himself at the same time. "Bliss. Today in council. You met with a man named Bliss?"

Vennemann leaned away from Werner's spittling mouth. "Now that you are American, you cannot hold your lager, Werner?"

Werner shoved him, throwing himself backward into something soft and vocal. Stepping forward to Vennemann, he shouted again, "Bliss! Steamboat clerk. Titian Something Bliss."

"Werner, I don't know—"

"Charles said he was at a meeting with the council. Why would he be there?"

Vennemann gripped Roebling a little closer. He looked around and let out a small laugh, like he was catching up to a joke. "All we did today was approve the bridge issue. Not *all.*" He smiled at Roebling. "That's going to be the biggest bridge in the world, Werner, right here."

Roebling coughed. "Longest suspension bridge."

Vennemann nodded. "Exactly."

Werner sagged against a nearby table, jostling the drinks. He stared down at his hands, narrowing one eye to steady things.

"This Bliss, he might have been there to spit on Connors and Greenwood," Vennemann said, a hopeful lilt in his voice. "First and third wards? The steamboaters could not be happy those two finally came around to the bridge."

Roebling tutted. "Even after I change the design for them, take out the center column, they think this bridge will do them harm. Well, if one plan won't do, another must. And Amos tells me they are no longer a problem."

Werner belched. "Amos?"

"And they are not, Mr. Roebling, they are not." Vennemann lifted his stein at the stern bridgemaker's face. "The vote has been taken. We'll have your bridge up—I only wish it led somewhere other than Kentucky."

Werner lurched forward and curled his fists around the

lapels of Roebling's vest. "What Amos?"

Roebling, shrinking from Werner's fiery attention, looked quickly to Vennemann, then down to his still-full beer, which had sloshed over onto his woolen sleeve, and finally back to the hulking man in front of him. "Amos Shinkle."

Werner's hands dropped to his side. He scowled like he stood over something rancid.

Vennemann reached over and patted at Roebling's chest, smoothing out the bunches left from Werner's fists. "Shinkle. If money smells bad, that man is stinking, and it'll only get riper when the tolls from that bridge start coming in."

"Ten years with my plan for the bridge and nothing," Roebling said. "Great men are considered thus because they willed and accomplished something great. Amos joins the Company this year, and now we begin building in six months."

"The Company?" Werner spat.

Roebling looked again to Vennemann and then back at Werner. "The Covington and Cincinnati Bridge Company? Amos Shinkle is its new president."

14
The Carriagemen

The *biergarten* turned on its side, and Werner spilled out across the cobblestones of Liberty like whiskey from an open jug. He veered right on Main Street, ran straight down the city's gullet.

Werner saw the path in his head, a cleavered pass through the city he had walked nearly every day since landing in Cincinnati three years before. The straight line of Main Street connected Over the Rhine to the river. The river funneled from Cincinnati to New Orleans. The port of New Orleans reached out and was touched by the world.

The street rose in an unexpected and disjointed rhythm, colliding with his feet as he urged them forward. The tepid, still waters they called the Rhine passed under him in four heavy strides. He drew great ragged heaves of breath. The wind that met his face felt cool at first, but soon oppressed him like a steaming, damp ligature that closed up his throat. Buildings tilted toward him, then receded into shadow before he could recognize them. Top-hatted pedestrians saw him coming and got out of the way—otherwise he bowled them over.

He looked down to find his hands gripping his knees, a pendulum of spittle swinging from his mouth. Sweat made his shirt heavy. Nausea rose in his throat. He ran again, holding an arm straight out to balance himself, like a tightrope walker rushing his routine.

The cobblestones ended, and Werner saw patches of the river through the garbled mass of steamboats ahead of him. He felt a sudden tightness and knew, before he did anything else, he would have to piss. He pitched down the slope of the Landing, slowing as hard-packed dirt turned to mud, splashing into the water, pushing straight legs forward until he raised a hand and slapped it against the chipped hull of a beached steamboat. With his other hand, he frantically twisted at the buttons on his pants.

Unburdened, Werner felt the river's wake, sour and warm like just-pulled milk, lick at his knees and shrink his trousers into a tight, clinging bunch around his shins. He pushed forward, downriver, ducking under gangways, trying to steady the wooden river monsters towering over him in his gaze long enough to identify the *High Water*. In a sudden jerk his elbow and face hit the river, and he was sitting in its sodden embrace. It felt so good he thrust fistfuls of the muddied liquid at his face. Enough of it got in his mouth to have him standing again and spitting it out, wringing out his gums.

A whiskey would help. The sun was making its merciful retreat behind the river, and the saloons would be full—newly made money spilling out with the beer and the blood. Werner cast a glance over his shoulder toward Rat's Row.

His mouth salivated in anticipation, but he turned again to the steamboats. His only company on the Landing was the sound of filthy river water purling through his boots as he loped along.

When he came alongside the *High Water*, Werner swayed while willing the blue letters and their red outlines to congeal into steady words. When enough of them seemed to be in the right place, he charged up the plank, landing on his elbows in the forecastle. He looked up, anticipating the pale, disapproving Jesse, but saw only the glow of lanterns from the boiler deck parlor.

Werner lurched into the darkness of the main deck, past the enormous boiler tanks and the bins of dusty coal predestined to be burned—chunks of ancient life graverobbed and sold and incinerated, sending up an angry eulogy of steam that would propel this boat south and back again. Werner worked his way deeper, searching out the staircase that would lead him up. Uselessly, he squinted against the darkness. His mouth sagged open, and he swung his arms, blocking unseen assailants. A pale rectangular glow grew ahead, and he ran to it. The patch of light heaved and bobbed like a dinghy in rough seas. Werner, caught in the depths, stared up at it. He pitched forward when his boot struck darkness made solid, and his forearms landed painfully, propping his body at an upward angle. He swore, but he had found the stairs. Up he clattered, each step illuminated more fully by the yellow-tinted light spilling down the stairway from above.

At the top of the stairs, Werner saw the glass door to the parlor and ran to it, planning to barge in, not planning. The door and its rippled glass shook violently in its frame when Werner hit it, but gave no ground.

A muted voice said from the parlor, “It’s a pull.”

Werner spent a moment parsing these words. He gave the door a testing yank, and it swung out at him. He walked into the room as welcome as a draft. Sitting alone at a round table, like a schoolboy left to finish his vegetables, Titian Ramsay Bliss glared up at him. Werner moved toward him, dodging the garish flotsam of highbacked chairs and draped table linens leaving a cluttered path in his wake.

Bliss yelled over his shoulder, “It’s Bosenbach. He’s alone.” His voice rang with practiced authority, but he stood and took a half step backward.

Werner shoved aside a chair blocking his way. It tipped, and one of its knuckled legs protruded into his path. His wrists hit the floor right before his face, and he groaned.

Bliss watched Werner writhe and reach for something steady to lift himself with. “And I believe he’s drunk.”

“Drunk?” Werner managed to right himself amongst the wreckage of tableware around him. “I am here to—” Werner shut his mouth and closed his right eye to clarify the vision of Amos Shinkle and his hired man, Guss, emerging from one of the cabins adjoining the salon.

“Why *are* you here, Bosenbach?” Shinkle asked. He moved to the table where Bliss stood and claimed a chair.

Guss stayed close to the exterior wall, approaching Werner’s right flank. Werner flipped open his right eye, opening the room into a confused forest of furred outlines. He felt the bile filling his throat and quickly wrenched down his left eye. When the worst of the nausea passed, he felt able to speak.

“For a bridge? For a bridge you killed him?” Werner saw something dark at the end of one of Guss’ arms. If the man would relax, or holster, Werner could draw on him.

"No one killed anyone," said Bliss, holding his arms out, trying to coax the situation down like a growling dog.

There was a clap, and Werner's loose arms flew up, elbows first, a marionette dancing a ridiculous jig. He saw Bliss' hips splay to the right, then his side erupted, laying out blood and viscera amongst polished chinaware. Through the gunshot's echo, Werner could hear Bliss screaming. Shinkle tilted back in his chair, and Guss strode over, holding a pistol leaking smoke. Guss took aim and shot again, this time through Bliss' mouth. Werner's hand fell to his hip to lift his pistol, but found only an empty holster. He saw a flash of Bettina pointing the revolver at him and gasped. He had left the gun with her at Grammer's.

"Reaching for your tobacco, there, Dutch?" Guss watched Werner grope at his hip. "No matter how much you pattycake it, won't make it give up a gun."

Shinkle let the front feet of his chair smack the floor. "Damnit all, Guss. Was that the plan?"

"This'll work even better. Dutch kills this one—" Guss nodded down at Bliss. "We heard the shots from outside, come in, and find him robbing the place—"

Shinkle inspected his shirtfront, lifting his jacket away and pulling at the fabric. He sighed heavily and lifted his hand toward Guss. On his shirt cuff, white protruding under his dark coat, was a large bloodstain. "Now, look."

Guss stared off into a corner. A haze of gunsmoke swam around gilded chandeliers and snaked toward drafty exits.

"Do you know where I get these shirts?"

"Of course I know. You tell me near every day," Guss snapped.

Shinkle looked at him like another stain on his sleeve, then leaned his head toward the corpse. "So much blood."

Guss shrugged and tilted his head. "Usual amount."

Werner still clutched at the air where the handle of his revolver should have been. The gunshots had sobered him enough to see through two eyes.

Guss considered him for a moment before holstering his pistol.

"Bosenbach." Shinkle looked up at Werner with something close to admiration in his voice. "The widow has paid you. What are you doing here?"

Werner swayed, but his words were steady. "She will pay more for your death."

"Not the man that keeps her business afloat." He grinned at Werner. "Afloat? Oh, don't be so Dutch. I own the debt on this boat. Substantial debt." Shinkle leaned back, eliciting a groan from his chair. "This has been a week, Bosenbach. Quite a week. When I am old and bedridden, I'll remember this time."

Werner took a step forward. "You killed Dell Walker."

"Dell Walker killed Dell Walker."

"It was no accident."

"Only progress. Do you know who Robert Fulton was?"

Guss rolled his eyes and looked away.

"*Nein.*"

"He is the reason you're here." The blood on his shirtsleeve caught Shinkle's eye. He sighed and shook his head, then leaned back and slapped his thighs. "I am not a man for these fancy parlors, Bosenbach. There's a view outside. Let's take it in."

Werner wanted to say no, but he could think of no good response other than strangling the man. He shrugged. "*Ja.* OK."

Outside, on the hurricane deck that surrounded the

parlor, Shinkle gripped the railing in two fists like the reins of a horse and spoke as soon as Werner caught up with him. "Papin, Hulls, Fitch—you don't hear about them. You hear about Robert Fulton. Don't believe everything you hear. Fulton did not invent the steamboat, but he did even better: he brought it to America. And bringing it here, he made this country small, tamed it. My daddy's time, this was the ends of God's Earth. Harder to get to than heaven for a sinner, and then once you're here? A piece of land surrounded by savages likely to skin you alive." Shinkle flung out his right hand, upriver. "Our plot was only a couple dozen miles that way. Robert Fulton brung me from there. Brung us all to here." Shinkle nodded at the city, winking candlelit glass and gray shapes in the night.

Werner could feel the great wooden mass beneath his feet rise and fall like a shirt covering the sleeping chest of the river.

Guss stepped out of the parlor, lightly whistling and reloading his pistol.

Shinkle continued, pointing up the river. "Get here from New York, Pittsburgh, Philadelphia." His hand moved west. "Or, against the river, get here from New Orleans, easy. From Dublin and Hamburg, too."

Werner sighed. "This is a long story."

"Mhmm," intoned Guss.

Shinkle ignored them both. "Fulton brung all this," he waved at the city and turned to look at Werner, leaning on the railing, "but what of the carriagemen?"

Werner hiccupped. "The what?"

Shinkle looked at Werner, glass-eyed and swaying, drew in a breath to speak, then stopped. He turned back to the view. "You're right, Guss, there's no speaking with these

Dutch. Just go on."

The killer's resting smirk dropped into nothing. The pistol shots cracked the stillness of the night's air, echoing over the Landing, dying over the river.

15
The Guarantee

One shot.

It sounded faint to Werner, and he felt nothing but what he usually felt: a dull, simmering anger and an urge for a drink.

Two shots.

Werner had hoped, in this moment, he would see his father's creased hand, stretched out and waiting to pull him up. Or wise, warm men in robes, like the Hammer spoke of. Instead, he thought of the man he had sat next to in that saloon. Someone walked in and without a word, shot the man in the head. They had his brain wiped up and his seat filled with another roustabout before the ringing had left Werner's ears.

Three shots.

The glass behind him broke and made a din around his feet. Werner unclenched his eyes and lifted his head, lowering his arms from his face. He saw Shinkle huddled behind the deck railing, yelling something. Guss stood, holding his gun, but he had it pointed out at Cincinnati, at all the buildings and lighted windows and people dreaming, awake or sleeping. Werner saw the man aim his pistol at all of it, the detritus filling this basin that sloped toward the river, and felt a surge of sympathy for the killer—a man with a gun arrayed against the idea that we made the world better by making it more human. Then the revolver erupted.

Werner followed Guss' aim in time to see a muzzle flash rending the night's fabric. It revealed Bettina's face. Her eyes were squeezed shut against the violence roaring from Werner's gun in her hands. In the same instant she was illuminated, the night swallowed her whole, leaving the vision of her just a green halo behind Werner's eyelids.

Werner now understood Guss was aiming at Bettina, and Bettina was aiming right back. He charged at the killer, but stopped short when he saw Charles behind Guss, moving toward them along the hurricane deck with his arm raised. Charles brought his hand down, and Guss fell. The two men eyed each other, Werner swaying, Charles' chest expanding and contracting, until another gunshot rang from the Landing.

"*Scheisse*, Bettina!" Werner yelled into the night.

They could hear her footfalls descend the Landing toward the boat, and it was the only thing they heard until Shinkle stood and started to yell.

"Boy, do you know—you've assaulted a white man," Shinkle cried. "You can't just—do you know what's going to—you could dream about hanging, but I wouldn't get my hopes up."

Werner ignored Shinkle's outburst, and looked down at Guss, blood leaking from the back of his head where

Charles' blackjack had landed. "Where have you been?" he asked Charles.

"I was asleep down below. That whiskey you brought had me looking for a berth in the main deck. Heard you bumbling and crashing around, thought you was some drunk in the wrong place. By the time I got my pants on, I heard shots and voices and came to take a look."

"I am drunk, but in the right place." Werner pointed at Shinkle. "They killed Captain Dell to build a bridge."

Shinkle extended a finger at Werner. "Now—"

"I heard enough to know," said Charles.

"Know? What do you know? Either of you? Here is what you are going to do. You," Shinkle pointed at Charles, "you stop up that bleeding on Guss' head. And best send up a couple prayers he don't remember you hitting him. When he gets an idea of killing a man, it usually ends up that way. And you," Shinkle swung his arm to Werner, "get on back in that parlor and dispose of poor Bliss."

Werner cocked his head. "Dispose?"

"Take away. Get rid of. You Dutch don't hardly bother to even learn the language, do you?"

The three men turned toward the sound of footsteps hammering up the stairs. Bettina emerged and collided with Werner with enough force to expel the air from his lungs. She hit the back of his head with the still-hot barrel of his pistol when she threw her arms around his neck and bloodied his lip with a kiss that landed like a jab. It tasted like iron, felt like a bee sting, and then it was gone.

Bettina pressed her head against his chest. "I came after you, but I couldn't catch up," she said. "I didn't know where you were. Then I heard a man talking and saw you up here, and he was going to shoot you."

Werner felt her hands fall away across his shoulders and saw her face go to ash at the sight of Guss' prone figure.

"I killed him," Bettina said, equal parts wonder and broken despair.

"You didn't kill him, Miss," said Charles. "I did."

With that, Charles plucked from his pocket a two-barreled derringer, hardly visible engulfed by his hand, and fired both rounds into Guss' chest. Werner jumped back at the gun's reports, like something wet landing on cobblestone from a great height. Shinkle opened his mouth and drew in a yelling-sized breath, but said nothing. He nodded slightly to himself.

Charles pointed at Werner and Bettina. "You my two witnesses. He tried—"

Shinkle held out a conciliatory hand. "There won't be any need for that." He looked down at Guss, cocking his head in alignment with the dead man's. He exhaled and closed his eyes and kept nodding.

Werner was suddenly aware of the night sounds around them—crickets shrieking and frogs calling—and he imagined they were all yelling at each other, arguing over a way to stop up whatever dam burst and let out all these people.

Shinkle's head snapped up, his eyes wide and cold. "I owe you both thanks."

Charles and Werner glanced at each other.

Shinkle pointed at Guss' still form. "That man was a menace. Out of control." Shinkle shook his head. "Corrupt. If I can tell you the truth, he scared me."

Werner spit. "Bettina," he said, "give me the gun."

She looked down, surprised to find it still viced into her hand. She nearly threw it at him.

Opening the cylinder, Werner found one shot left.

"Enough in here for you," he said to Shinkle.

"I am a victim, Bosenbach." Shinkle tugged down at his waistcoat, arranging himself, straightening and finding the timbre of his voice. "A victim of my own trusting nature."

Werner lifted the pistol at him.

The words scurried from Shinkle's mouth. "I can help you." He swept a hand across the damaged boat, and the two bleeding bodies it held. "With this. And you, boy," Shinkle turned to Charles, pleading, "I can—"

"My name is Charles," he said.

Werner drew back the hammer.

"Of course," Shinkle said. "Charles. Charles, I can help you, too. I own this boat now, in all the ways that matter. If you continue to take on passengers who, who," Shinkle struggled for the words, "... don't pay for their passage? That would be—well, after Bosenbach told the widow that her husband was killed by a slave hunter, that may be more than you'd get from her. But you kill me, there's no knowing who will buy this boat. Maybe Gillespie or Nichols. Gillespie, most like. And he wouldn't stand for any of that."

"*Backpfeifengesicht*," Bettina said.

Werner coughed up a wet laugh. He translated for Shinkle, "She says you have a face that wants punching."

"Tough women you Dutch bring with you," Shinkle said with a weak laugh.

"I was born here," Bettina said, no trace of German in her accent.

"Even tougher, then," Shinkle said. He smiled at Bettina, who showed no sign of having heard him. "I've been told that before, about my face, you know. Not quite like that, but." He clutched at his goatee. "Have you all thought about what's coming next?"

Bettina nodded toward Werner. “He shoots you. We go home and have a lager.”

Shinkle never took his eyes from the open end of the pistol Werner had pointed at his face. “That does sound good. But well, now, justice, she’s blind, but that don’t count the men she subcontracts to. They see pretty good. And if you shoot me, they’ll see three dead white men. A chief clerk,” he nodded toward the parlor then pointed at his own chest, “a city councilman, and,” he gestured down at Guss with his eyes, “a United States marshal.”

“Marshal?” Werner and Charles said in unison.

“August—Guss—Sturges.” Shinkle cringed, narrowing his eyes. “Dirtier than the bottom of your boot, but a marshal, still.” He looked at each of them, looking at him. “You must have known that.”

Charles and Bettina turned to Werner, who shrugged while maintaining his unsteady aim at Shinkle.

Shinkle said, “So, they’ll see three dead white men, and not just river workers, but real white men. Someone has to answer that bell.” He looked at each of them in turn. “And who better than a nigger and a pair of the damned Dutch?”

Werner made the decision to shoot him, raising the pistol from Shinkle’s chest to his face.

Shinkle held up his hands. “Not my words, just what they’ll say.”

“And if he doesn’t shoot you?” Bettina asked.

Shinkle smiled crookedly at her. “Yes, tough and smart. Yes, say Bosenbach does not shoot me. Then I am able to tell my friends—on both sides of this river—about his heroics here tonight. I tell them about a corrupt marshal who killed Dell Walker and Bliss in there and would have killed me were it not for Boomin’ Bosenbach.” Shinkle turned to

Werner. "That's a story they'll believe, if I'm the one telling it. One the papers might even want. And Charles," Shinkle said, gesturing to the other man, "he goes on doing his good work on this boat. You, Miss," he said to Bettina, "you get to go back home and have a lager. So, shooting me or not shooting me, I suppose it's just about the same for you."

"And you get your bridge," said Werner.

"I get to go home to my son," Shinkle replied. Then he pointed back at the lights of Cincinnati. "They get the bridge."

Werner still wanted to shoot him. The gun permeated warmth through the palm of his hand, yearning to be fired.

"He's right, Boom," said Charles, nearly under his breath.

Werner only realized the fierce clench of his jaw when he let it relax. He felt Bettina's hand guiding his gun down to his side. Looking at his feet, it took him three tries to holster the pistol.

"*Ja*, he said finally. "OK."

The next day, Bettina had to fill in the numerous gaps in Werner's memory, while he tried to squeeze the ache out of his head.

"We let him go?"

She tangled her fingers in his and nodded. "It was really that Sturges who killed Captain Walker," she said.

"Shinkle plans it all and tells him what to do, and I get Sturges." Werner held his head between his knees for a long moment. "I need to go to Covington."

Bettina look at him, startled. "You can't go kill—"

Werner shook his head. "I am not going to kill," he said. "But you come with me, make sure I don't."

Across the river, standing under a shading tree, Bettina watched Werner climb the wooden stairs of Sophia Walker's porch. He seemed ready to knock, but instead thrust his hand into a coat pocket and drew out his fist filled with bills. He bent over, slid them under the widow's door, and walked back down the stairs.

When Werner told Lafcadio about the money he had returned to Sophia Walker, the Irishman laughed long and loud. Then he docked Werner an extra thirty dollars to cover his end of the missing cash. After that, when Lafcadio was selling Werner's services to people who had read about him in papers—twice, now—he'd always promise with a leering smile: "Boomin' Bosenbach'll have your man, *guaranteed.* Or your money back. Less the expenses, sure."

Werner and Bettina meandered together through the streets of Covington. It wasn't until they were on the ferry going back north that Werner spoke. He looked out at the water that rushed around them, that the ferry fought through to take them back. What was stuck and swallowed and drowned in its rushing eddies? He wondered where it came from, the mud that made the river brown, that shaped new turns and built new banks. What new direction did the river take because of that silt?

"I'm thirsty," he said.

ABOUT THE AUTHOR

Chris Geier lives in western Massachusetts with his wife and children. This is his first book.

AUTHOR THANKS

My deepest thanks and gratitude to:

Leah Angstman for taking a chance on this book, and everyone at Alternating Current for your help in making it better.

The Cincinnati Public Library, for its excellent research resources, and for a quiet place where the first words of this book were written. The Cincinnati History Library and Archives, for its wealth of primary sources and scholarly articles, which helped form the story's historical backbone.

The Yale Writer's Workshop for providing a place to work on an early draft of this book, and to the excellent writers and instructors there who provided a young writer with guidance and advice.

My family. Mom and Dad, Elizabeth and Kate, I love you. GG, you're an inspiration; thank you for opening my eyes and heart to Cincinnati.

Flannery. The most. Always.

COLOPHON

The edition you are holding is the First Edition of this publication.

The heavy font used throughout the book is Wicked Grit, created by A. J. Paglia. The subfont used throughout the book is The Goldsmith Vintage, created by Burntilldead Typefoundry. All other text is set in Marion, created by Ray Larabie, based on vintage press plates. The Alternating Current Press logo is Portmanteau, created by JLH Fonts. All fonts used with permission; all rights reserved.

Front and back cover artwork created by Leah Angstman from public-domain images and maps of Cincinnati in the 1850s. Special thank you to Dustin Marks at Cincy Map Collection for making copies accessible to the public.

The hat graphic is from the Gentleman Icons set, created by Woodcutter.

The publisher wishes to thank Alexander Knetsch for his aid in German language accuracy.

The Alternating Current lightbulb logo was created by Leah Angstman, ©2013, 2020 Alternating Current. Chris Geier's photo was taken by Max Yeager, ©2020. All material used with permission; all rights reserved.

OTHER WORKS FROM
Alternating Current Press

All of these books (and more) are available at
Alternating Current's website: press.alternatingcurrentarts.com.

alternatingcurrentarts.com

Made in the USA
Middletown, DE
17 February 2020